The Second Book of Old Mermaids Tales

Also by Kim Antieau

Old Mermaids Books

The Annotated Church of the Old Mermaids
The Blue Tail • Church of the Old Mermaids
The First Book of Old Mermaids Tales • The Fish Wife
Magic, Myth, and Merrymaking: 13 Days of Yuletide the Old Mermaids Way • An Old Mermaid Journal
The Old Mermaids Book of Days and Nights
The Old Mermaids Book of Days and Nights: A Year and a Day Journal • The Old Mermaids Mystery School
The Old Mermaids Oracle • The Old Mermaids Wisdom Cards
Spirits, Spells, and Storytelling: 13 Days of Hallows the Old Mermaids Way

Other Novels

Broken Moon • Butch • Coyote Cowgirl • Deathmark
The Desert Siren • Her Frozen Wild • The Gaia Websters
Jewelweed Station • The Jigsaw Woman • Killing Beauty
Mercy, Unbound • The Monster's Daughter
Queendom: Feast of the Saints • The Rift • Ruby's Imagine
Swans in Winter • Whackadoodle Times
Whackadoodle Times Two • Whackadoodle Times Three
Whackadoodle Times Galore

Other Nonfiction

Answering the Creative Call
Certified: Learning to Repair Myself and the World in the Emerald City • Counting on Wildflowers: An Entanglement
MommaEarth Goddess Runes
The Salmon Mysteries: a Reimagining of the Eleusinian Mysteries
Under the Tucson Moon: Nine Winters in the Sonoran Desert

The Second Book of Old Mermaids Tales

Kim Antieau

Green Snake
PUBLISHING

For MaryAnn

Contents

Introduction

This morning I was up with the sun and out on the Sanctuary. The monsoon has given us an abundance of plant and animal life.

On my walk around this wild and unique slice of desert, I saw several rabbits. They remained as still as rocks until I got too close. Then they ran off, their white tails bouncing like rubber balls behind them.

Later I saw a snakeskin at the corner of the barn. It was left there by a small rattlesnake after molting. I didn't pick it up. Didn't want a couple of fangs chomping on my hand.

As I neared the Quail House, I heard the soft rolling clicks of a roadrunner calling for its mate, no doubt. It was out of my sight, but I suspect its intended knew exactly where it was.

In the Quail House, I found an enormous spider in the

window air conditioning unit. It seemed to like its home there and I let it be. Who am I to tell it where it should and should not live?

Beneath the overhang of our porch, a dove looked down on me with steady black eyes from its wild and woolly nest. We can expect some baby doves in a week or two.

I opened the gate by the pool and beheld an enormous and gorgeous feat of engineering: a spider's web at least three feet in diameter with the engineer herself stationed at the center awaiting a passing meal that I was sure would come soon. I stepped back, out of respect and admiration, and found another way into the patio.

A row of ants carried the petals that had fallen from a barometer bush in a stately animated line across the ground, like flowers marching to their own rhythm.

Lizards criss-crossed my path, moving like lightning in all directions, a storm of dust and frantic motion.

The numerous fishhook barrel cactuses were all crowned with startlingly beautiful orange and red blossoms dusted with powdery yellow pollen. Hummingbirds would soon be on them, not to mention bees and other pollinators.

I felt as though the Sanctuary was really living up to its name. So much life finds refuge here. Kim and I wanted this place to be home to the wild things, and that is how it has turned out.

On other days we see coyotes, javelinas, and bobcats. Gila monsters, mice, and frogs. Vermillion flycatchers, cardinals, and cactus wrens. Sometimes it seems the life here is endless.

The Old Mermaids, I was sure, would delight in this bounty of life just as much as I did. After all, the Sanctuary is life following art. The Old Ems first appeared in Kim's novel *Church of the Old Mermaids*, which she wrote on this land in the Quail House. That book describes how they had to leave the Old Sea when it dried up and how they washed ashore onto the New Desert.

They were sad to leave their home, but they learned to survive and thrive in the desert. They learned new ways to live and became a part of their community. They created a Sanctuary in the desert and welcomed all visitors.

Now Kim and I are stewards and guardians of land very much like the land in the novel. We revel in the wild creatures that inhabit it with us. We maintain the land and plants for the benefit of all that come here.

This doesn't mean the Old Mermaids are no longer here. Far from it. They are with us constantly. Their spirit guides us and informs us.

When we have to decide what to do with a weed or a tree that grows where we don't expect it, we ask what the Old Mermaids would do in the same situation.

We don't always get an answer, but thinking about life from their perspective often gives us all we need.

The Old Mermaids are full of stories, and they love to tell them. In this second collection of their tales, Kim has gathered some of their most entertaining and enlightening yarns.

The Old Mermaids are accepting and full of wisdom. They support each other and look for the best in everyone. They don't *always* find what they are looking for, but they wouldn't live life any other way.

Dive into these stories with an open heart and hopeful attitude. You won't be disappointed.

Blessed Sea!

—Mario Milosevic
27 August 2022

The Old Mermaids and the Hummingbirds

On the Old Mermaids Sanctuary, Sister Ruby Rosarita Mermaid was just as fascinated with hummingbirds as all of the Old Ems and the Old Neighbors were, but she knew that some of the hummingbirds were more than they at first appeared. I can't be certain if she ever told this story to anyone else besides the other Old Mermaids—probably, since she was a good storyteller—but it also felt like a secret to her.

One spring day, a storm came up over the Mountains. It was strange because they had heard no rumblings from any of the creatures or the Wind or the Sky. Even Myka Summers didn't mention that her dog Bay had howled or not because that dog bayed every time a storm was near.

And one of the Old Neighbors usually had a bit of an asthma attack just before a fierce storm, and she felt fine all the day long.

But the storm broke over the Mountains, dumping monsoon-like rain down the slopes that eventually flowed into the creeks, washes, and river beds. Lightning streaked ahead of the storm and behind it, as though it was leading or herding the storm.

Sister Faye Mermaid watched it and predicted, "This is someone else's magic, not ours. We best go into the house."

And so they all did, except Sister Ruby Rosarita Mermaid who stayed on the edge of the wash a few moments longer. Three things happened all at once: two hummingbirds flew past her, flying low in the wash, but not so fast that Sister Ruby Rosarita Mermaid didn't spot the yellow pollen on their beaks; it began raining in sheets; and water came coursing down the dry arroyo, filling it almost instantly, tossing and turning like a miniature ocean during a fierce storm.

Sister Ruby Rosarita Mermaid was about to turn and run inside—since she was soaked through and through—when she heard splashing in the wash. She looked to her left and saw two tall faeries—as tall as the pine tree next to the house—walking through the running water. They were laughing as their purple and green silk shirts and pants got drenched. They both had green hair, gold skin, and one blue and one brown eye—and something bright yellow powdered their noses.

Sister Ruby Rosarita Mermaid waved. The faeries stopped amidst the tumult of rain and water and wind and faery laughter and looked down at her.

"An Old Em!" the one with the darkest gold skin said. "I've always wanted to meet one. How do you do?"

"I do fine," she shouted.

"Give her the present," the dark gold skin one said.

The other faery pulled something out of its feather-trimmed pocket, something small and round and golden. The faery bent over and opened its palm. On it sat a yellow cake.

The other faery bent over too. "It's a yellow pollen cake. The bees left the pollen with our mother when she asked them what the druids know. They told her all you need is in Nature."

"Take it," the offering faery said. "May you all know nourishment all the days and nights of your lives."

Sister Ruby Rosarita Mermaid took the cake from the faery's hand. It vibrated on her palm and smelled like she imagined poppies would smell if they decided to have a scent.

"Thank you," Sister Ruby Rosarita Mermaid said.

"Thank you for letting us be ourselves," they sang. "OK?"

The faeries stood up straight. The rain stopped, and

the new river began quickly receding. Just like that, the faeries were hummingbirds again, flying away from her.

Sister Ruby Rosarita Mermaid said, "Now I know where birds go in the rain. They turn into faeries."

She hurried into the house, and all the Old Mermaids had many helpings of the Faery Bee Pollen Cake and felt nourished all the days of their lives.

Kim Antieau

In the Beginning

When Myla Alvarez first started the Church of the Old Mermaids—after the dream—she saved the money she earned. It wasn't much, but it was something, and she knew she would figure out what to do with it eventually. Then one day during a trip out into the desert searching for treasure, she saw a group of people in the sandy bottom of an old wash. She went over to say hello. Three men, a boy, and a woman sat on the dirt, too exhausted to move. She immediately offered water. They gave it to the woman, who was barely conscious. Myla wanted to take them to the hospital, but they refused. Once they drank the water and ate the food she gave them, they revived. They had crossed the border illegally, as she guessed, and had been deserted by their smuggler—the *guia*—soon after they crossed. Myla took them to her apartment in the Crow barn, fed them, and let them use her phone. The woman—Grace—was too ill to leave with the others, so Myla let her and her son, Roberto, stay. She didn't give it a second thought. She got her keys and took them over to the Ford place and let them sleep there. The Old Mermaids Sanctuary—in its present form—was born.

Two days later, using some of the money she had earned from the Church of the Old Mermaids, Myla bought Grace and Roberto bus tickets to Texas where Grace's husband worked in the fields. After she took them to the bus station, Myla came home and went to the Ford house to clean it, but the house was spotless, the garden tidy, the dirt raked. Myla believed the house felt better too. A house was created to be lived in. That was its purpose. When the Fords returned, they even re-marked that the place had never looked better.

Myla kept making excursions to the desert, near *la frontera*. Sometimes she found people, sometimes she did not. She was very careful about who she brought home with her and even more careful about who she let stay in the houses. When she told her friend Theresa what she was doing, Theresa offered to help. Myla was glad to have her as a partner, especially since Theresa was a private investigator and many of the migrants came looking for family, friends—and a job. After a while, Theresa and Myla began going into the desert to-gether, mostly in the summer when it was so dangerous

                                              Kim Antieau

for those crossing. In recent years, they sometimes encountered other rescuers who left water or transported migrants to the hospital, all activities which had been deemed legal until recently. A few months earlier a couple had been arrested as they drove several people to an area hospital. They were charged with aiding and abetting illegal aliens. Or something like that. Myla knew if she got caught, she wouldn't be able to help anyone, so she and Theresa kept quiet about what actually went on at the Old Mermaids Sanctuary, and they avoided the other rescuers as much as possible.

In the winter, the Sanctuary was usually quiet, except for visits from the homeowners. Summer was busier. Myla made certain each house was not occupied often or for very long, and visitors always did work around the property in exchange for their room and board. One year a family retiled the Castillo roof. Another time, a man helped fix the gray water irrigation system at the Ford house. Myla told the migrants that if anyone happened to see them and ask what they were doing there, they were to say that Myla had hired them. After all, the homeowners had instructed her to keep up the yards, facilitate repairs, and make the houses looked lived in. Myla made certain all that happened—only the workers stayed in the houses while they did the work.

Myla kept an Old Mermaids Sanctuary binder. In it, she put photos of the visitors with their names, ages, which house they had stayed in and what work they had done. Almost always, the migrants sent Myla a postcard once they were settled, and she'd add those to the binder.

Myla understood that these niceties would not placate the owners should they ever learn of her venture. She knew they would view what she was doing as a betrayal. Criminal even. She knew she could not adequately explain her actions; she could not tell them that the Old Mermaids had come to her in a dream and that she was doing their work here on dry land. That would sound crazy. Or—at the very least—possessed. She had tried to figure out other ways to explain what she had done— what she was doing. It wasn't like she thought God had spoken to her, or that she was channeling Ramtha or that she'd seen a vision of the Virgin Mary. It was more like the Invisibles of the land—and the sea—had spoken to her. But that wasn't right either. The land and its occupants were always speaking and she just happened to be able to understand them one morning a decade ago. Now she always heard them, in the form of the stories that poured from her mouth like a wonderful kind of babel— or babble—which most people, fortunately, understood.

                                     Kim Antieau

Old Coyote: A Myla Alvarez Story

Two women walked up to the table first. One was older, probably the younger one's mother; they looked like one another. Myla had seen at least one of them before, but she didn't think she had ever known her name. Myla sipped her lemonade as they looked at the items on the table.

The older woman picked up a stuffed dog. "This looks like it's been in the wars."

Myla nodded. She had washed the dog, but it was still rather sad-looking.

"I don't imagine the Old Mermaids had stuffed animals," the woman said.

"They don't seem like they'd have a pile of stuffed animals on their beds, do they?" Myla said. "Well, except maybe for this one time. I can't be sure, but I think this might be the stuffed dog that belonged to Sister Sheila Na Giggles Mermaid. I know what you're going to say. Of all the Old Mermaids, Sister Sheila Na Giggles Mermaid seems like the least likely one to have a stuffed animal. She was probably the handiest and most practical of all the Old Mermaids. She could fix a plugged sink, a broken door, a leaky roof—all the while she told jokes. These were not ordinary every day Old Mermaid jokes. We know the Old Mermaids all had great senses of humor. They were good storytellers, the entire baker's dozen of them. But Sister Sheila Na Giggles Mermaid could make the moon blush with her jokes. Let us say her jokes had an energetic earthiness to them. By the way, that is the dictionary definition of raunch, so you get my point.

"Sometimes the whole neighborhood could hear the groans after Sister Sheila Na Giggles Mermaid told her jokes to the other Old Mermaids. The Old Neighbor and the Old Neighbor's Husband would look at each other and say, 'It must have been a good one. Sorry we missed it.' Or 'It must have been a bad one. Good thing we missed it. We'll have to have her tell it to us later.' I can't repeat any of her jokes here, but I will say they often involved Coyote and his adventures. They weren't scatological jokes. Nothing like that. But Sister Sheila Na Giggles Mermaid's coyote was often looking for some female coyote company.

                                        Kim Antieau

"Well, after Sister Sheila Na Giggles Mermaid had been telling these jokes for a while, the Old Mermaids noticed that a big old coyote began hanging around the Old Mermaids Sanctuary. He was raggedy-looking, I'm telling you. The Old Mermaids were accustomed to having coyotes on the sanctuary. They often saw them in the wash and heard them serenading the moon or the desert or themselves in the evening. This coyote had a torn ear, a scar down across one eye—although whatever scarred him seemed to have actually missed the eye; it just scarred his forehead and eyelid. He had a tuft of hair missing on one side, almost as though someone had tried to brand him. Sister Sheila Na Giggles Mermaid was a bit beat up herself. Sometimes when she was doing work on the house or out on the land, she would be talking and so involved in telling her jokes or stories that she'd miss the nail she was hammering and get her hand or get tangled up in rope or cable or her feet. She'd get the job done, mind you, but there was usually a bit of bloodletting. So when Sister Sheila Na Giggles Mermaid saw this Old Coyote, she took an immediate liking to him. After a while, she asked Sister Ursula Divine Mermaid if she knew why the coyote was hanging around. Sister Ursula Divine Mermaid had a way with our furred and feathered kind. So Sister Ursula Divine Mermaid went out to see what she would see about Old Coyote.

"When she came back, she told Sister Sheila Na Giggles Mermaid that Old Coyote was a bit more laconic than your average loquacious coyote. 'I think he's here because of your jokes,' Sister Ursula Divine Mermaid said. 'Oh,' Sister Sheila Na Giggles Mermaid said, 'do you think I've offended him?' 'Offend a coyote?' Sister Ursula Divine Mermaid said. 'Are you kidding? If you only knew what they were saying when they were out in the wash yipping away. No, I think he wants to hear some jokes himself.'

"The next few days, Sister Sheila Na Giggles Mermaid noticed that wherever she went, Old Coyote went. After a while, she just started talking out loud. 'Well, it's a beautiful day, isn't it, Old Coyote? Never seen a bluer morning. The birds are singing. The water is flowing. Somewhere. Somewhere water is flowing. It puts me in mind of this one morning Coyote woke up and found himself all alone. He was so lonely. Every night he howled at the stars and moon asking them to send him someone to keep him warm at night. And every night he shivered and curled up all alone. And then one night he was walking through the wash and he saw a cute little coyote under a mesquite, curled up on the tree's exposed roots. At least that's what he thought he saw. It was night, and his eyes weren't as good as they used to be. He went as close as he could get since he didn't want to chase her away, and he didn't want to get too close or she'd see that he wasn't the sleek young coyote he had

                                    Kim Antieau

once been. He began telling her how beautiful she was. She didn't respond, so he continued singing to her, telling her how lovely she was in the nonexistent moonlight and if she'd only let him he'd make her happy for the rest of the season, at least, maybe more, they'd have to see how it went. This particular old coyote didn't want to commit to anything, you see.

"'He went on and on like this all night, and she never responded. He was just about to take her silence as acquiescence and move closer when the sun came up and light filled the wash, including the spot under the mesquite where someone had left an old mop. Coyote had been trying all night to make love to an old mop. Coyote put his tail between his legs and hurried away in the hopes that no one had heard him. But, of course, everyone had heard him, and coyotes up and down the wash repeated his lovemaking words in their songs the next night and the next night and the next night.' Sister Sheila Na Giggles Mermaid looked over at the Old Coyote. She could have sworn he was laughing. 'See,' she said. 'I knew that was funny. Mother Star Stupendous didn't get it. She kept asking me all sorts of questions. How could he not know it was a mop, she wanted to know. I had to go get a mop, you know, one of those with the long tendrils, or octopus-arms. I guess you wouldn't know. You're a coyote. What would you do with a mop. I had the same reaction when I found out about them. I'm an Old Mermaid. What would I do with a mop? But in the desert they can come in handy.'

"And so the conversations went between Old Coyote and Sister Sheila Na Giggles Mermaid. She was ecstatic that she had a receptive audience for her jokes. They became a familiar couple through the Old Mermaids Sanctuary and beyond for a long time, Sister Sheila Na Giggles Mermaid and the Old Coyote.

"Then one morning Sister Sheila Na Giggles Mermaid went out and Old Coyote wasn't there. She looked all around for him, but he was nowhere to be found. She worried that he had died or been killed; all the Old Mermaids did. But after a few weeks, someone stopped by the Old Mermaids Sanctuary. After Sister Sheila Na Giggles Mermaid told him one of her jokes, he said that reminded him of a joke he'd heard from a woman down south a ways. She lived with an old coyote and everyone was sure he was telling her the jokes because she had no sense of humor before he came along. After the man left, the Old Mermaids gathered around Sister Sheila Na Giggles Mermaid and told her they were sorry Old Coyote had moved on. Sister Magdelene Mermaid gave her this stuffed dog, the one you're holding. At least I think it was that one. She started making it for her as soon as Old Coyote left, only she didn't call it a stuffed dog. She said it was a stuffed coyote. See how its tongue is hanging out. Like he's laughing. Sister Bea Wilder Mermaid pat-

                                        Kim Antieau

ted Sister Sheila Na Giggles Mermaid on the back while she looked at the stuffed coyote and said, 'Well, Sister Mermaid, I guess Old Coyote found himself another mop.' They all laughed, except Mother Star Stupendous Mermaid who still didn't get it. And life went on at the Old Mermaids Sanctuary. They say Sister Sheila Na Giggles Mermaid hung onto this stuffed coyote until they left the Sanctuary. After that it went from this person to that. Some say that Old Coyote whispers jokes to whoever owns this little stuffed canine. Maybe it's Old Coyote, but I think it's probably Sister Sheila Na Giggles Mermaid. Who knows? I do know that all the people who have had possession of this stuffed animal have been very funny people. At least I think it's this stuffed animal. I can't be sure."

Sister Magdelene Mermaid and The Tall Dark Figure

One night during Dark Moon, Sister Magdelene Mermaid walked through the wash. A breeze rustled through the dry hackberry bushes, pencil cholla, and mesquite. A Tall Dark Figure stopped a short distance from the Old Em.

"This will be the path of the Wild Hunt," Tall Dark Figure said. "Why are you here?"

"I prepare the path with my love," Sister Magdelene Mermaid said.

"This is the Wild Hunt," Tall Dark Figure said, the disgust not disguised in their voice. "Love has no place here. Don't you know the world is filled with evil and destruction and horror?"

"Love has a place everywhere," she said. "You think I don't understand the world because I still love? You are wrong. I still love because I understand the world. It's not a puppy love, although I do love puppies and I suppose that is actually puppy love. But my love is an action, it is a devotion. It means I stand for the world. Including those who have died. Haven't you ever loved?"

"Of course not! And any of the participants in the wild hunt could tear you to bits and take you to the Underworld with them," Tall Dark Figure said. "Does that not frighten you?"

"Sometimes," Sister Magdelene Mermaid said. "And sometimes it doesn't."

"What is that in your hand?" Tall Dark Figure asked. "It is light. We need no light at this time."

"It is stardust," Sister Magdelene Mermaid said, and she let some of it sprinkle down from her finger tips. Each particle seemed to pick up light from who knows where: the stars above, Sister Magdelene Mermaid's eyes. "We are all made from it, even you, Tall Dark Figure."

"I eat stardust for lunch," Tall Dark Figure said, "and poop out universes by dinner."

"That is quite a skill," Sister Magdelene Mermaid said. She held out her stardust-filled hands. "Would you like some now, tonight, so you can poop out more universes by morning?"

"You are a cheeky Old Em," Tall Dark Figure said. "If you are all so fearless, maybe you will survive the Wild Hunt, should you stumble into it."

"We are all different," Sister Magdelene Mermaid said.

"I don't have time for any more stardust talk."

"OK," Sister Magdelene Mermaid said. "If I see you during the Wild Hunt, I'll wave and say hello."

"We don't wave and say hello during the Wild Hunt," they said, sounding exasperated.

"What do you do then?"

"We are a horde of ravishers looking for souls to take," they said. "We don't wave. We don't say hello."

Sister Magdelene Mermaid laughed. "I will take note of that. But I may forget and wave anyway."

"Then you'll just draw attention to yourself and someone will snatch your soul."

"That doesn't sound fun," she said. "All right. I will take your advice. No waving or saying hello."

"It is not advice," they said. "I don't give advice." They shook their head. Then they walked by her in the wash. Their passing created a little breeze, and stardust wafted out of Sister Magdelene Mermaid's hands.

"Oh, it looks so beautiful on your black robes," Sister Magdelene Mermaid said.

"I am not beautiful!" they said as they kept walking. "Just stay hidden during it all."

"More advice!" Sister Magdelene Mermaid called. "You do love me!"

"I do not," they said. "I do not, I do not, I do—" and they disappeared into the night.

Sister Magdelene Mermaid smiled. "What a grumpy destructive goose," she said as she continued walking and letting loose stardust from her fingertips. "I wonder what one wears to a Wild Hunt?"

The Girl Who Didn't Speak and the Tea Party

One day, a young mother and her seven-year-old daughter stumbled into the Old Mermaids Sanctuary. Their eyes were glassy, their clothes torn and tattered, their shoes falling apart.

The Old Mermaids brought them food and drink, treated their cuts and scrapes, and took them indoors when they were ready.

The mother's name was Gimena, and the girl was called Ichika. After they had bathed and rested, they sat outside by the pool and garden, and Gimena told the Old Ems that they had come from a place of war. Her husband had been captured by gangs. As her husband was dragged away, he shouted, "I will meet you where the sea ends and the magic begins." Gimena feared they would come back for her and her daughter, so she left.

"I have been looking for a place where the sea ends and magic begins for many days and weeks now," Gimena said. With tears in her eyes, she asked, "Do you think this is the place? Have you seen my husband? His name is Ain. He has one blue eye and one brown eye. The grandmothers in our village used to say he was blessed and could see into two worlds at once. But the grandmothers are no more, and my husband is—" She glanced over at Ichika who sat near the pool staring into the bottom of it. She had not said a word since the Old Mermaids met her. "My husband is missing from our lives."

Grand Mother Yemaya Mermaid said, "We are so sorry for your troubles. This is a place where the Old Sea ended, and we have our share of magic. So perhaps this is the place. You are welcome to stay here as long as you like."

And so Gimena and her daughter Ichika came to live at the Old Mermaids Sanctuary for a time. Gimena helped the Old Mermaids out at the Tea Shell, where she served special teas, sopas, and desserts to all the Old Neighbors. At first Ichika stayed close to her mother, but after a while she also spent time with the Old Mermaids. She never said a word. She just stayed near, helping them out in the kitchen or garden or when they went to

                                        Kim Antieau

visit their neighbors. She went with them to birthday celebrations. She helped Sissy Maggie sew new clothes for them. At night sometimes, she sat with Mother Star Stupendous Mermaid and Grand Mother Yemaya Mermaid as they gazed up at the sky and pointed out stars to one another.

Still she said nothing.

One evening Ichika and Sister Laughs a Lot Mermaid were walking back from a community dinner at Annie Who Loves Birds' house. The other Old Mermaids and Gimena were either ahead of them or behind them. After a while Ichika and Sister Laughs a Lot Mermaid sat on the bench near the fork in the wash. It had been a long and tiring day.

La Luna rose in the sky, and it seemed suddenly and all at once and over an eon that silver light bathed the desert. Just then Ichika and Sister Laughs a lot Mermaid heard something peculiar. It sounded like the clinking of glass against glass or fork against plate.

What on Earth?

Ichika and Sister Laughs a Lot Mermaid got up and began walking quietly to the wash. The sound grew louder, and now they could hear voices. They went down into the wash and began walking. The dry river curved a bit. And then they saw it, in a stream of Moonlight, right there where they came to the fork in the wash: Sitting around a long wooden table with tea cups and platters of cookies and cupcakes and little sandwiches was a deer (or a deer woman), a jackrabbit or two, several bunny rabbits, a javelina, a pack rat, and a bobcat. They were all eating and drinking and talking, just like humans. In fact, they looked like people and animals all at the same time.

Sister Laughs a Lot Mermaid blinked and looked down at Ichika. Her eyes were wide. Sister Laughs a Lot Mermaid had seen many wondrous things in her life, but she had never seen a tea party with wild animals.

And these animals were dressed in the most ornate and beautiful clothes either of them had ever seen on any creature. The deer or woman wore a gold coat with all sorts of jewels catching the light and glittering each time she moved. Pack Rat or pack rat woman had on a purple top hat that matched her deep purple waistcoat. The jackrabbits and bunny rabbits only wore vests, but each vest was unique in its coloring and the design on the back. The javelina sported what looked like a pink velvet dress.

"This is the Deer Mother," Sister Laughs a Lot Mermaid whispered to Ichika. "I have heard stories of her."

The deer looked over at the Old Mermaid and the girl just then. "Ah, dear ones," she said. "Come. Join us."

Ichika looked up at Sister Laughs a Lot Mermaid who nodded. The two walked over to the table in the sand. Deer Mother pointed to the two empty chairs next to one another.

                    Kim Antieau

"We have been waiting for you," Deer Mother said. Sister Laughs a Lot Mermaid and Ichika sat on the wooden chairs with animals carved into every inch of them.

"We have?" Bobcat Man asked.

"We have," Jackrabbit said.

"Eat and drink," Javelina grumbled.

Sister Laughs a Lot Mermaid and Ichika both put goodies and sandwiches on their plates. They had never heard that one should not eat and drink in Fairyland or one might never be able to leave. Of course, some might argue that the Old Mermaids Sanctuary was part of Fairyland, hook, line, and sinker, as it were.

"I have never seen this before," Sister Laughs a Lot Mermaid said, "a table in the wash."

Deer Mother nodded. "I got tired of the wild life," she said. "So here we are."

The others around the table laughed. Sister Laughs a Lot Mermaid smiled and looked at Ichika who was biting into a chocolate cupcake.

"Beware, child," Deer Mother said. "Chocolate is powerful magic."

"Magic doesn't exist," Ichika said, her mouth filled with cupcake.

Ah, she had finally spoken.

Everyone around the table laughed again.

"Uh-oh," Bunny Rabbit said. "I guess that means I

don't exist." She snapped her fingers, and she disappeared. Ichika's eyes widened. Deer Mother snapped her fingers and Bunny Rabbit reappeared.

"Rude," Deer Mother said. "One mustn't disappear without notice."

And so they ate and told stories. Jackrabbit spoke about the many times he and his people danced in this same wash under the full Moon. Pack Rat remembered when the rancher destroyed her home. "It had been in my family for 40,000 years." Bobcat Man talked about the time his mother was killed by a hunter when he was just a cub. He barely survived. The others cried quietly when he described his life.

Then Deer Mother said, "We raise a cup to Bobcat Man's mother." They each held up their tea cup—including Ichika. "May Bobcat Man's mother continue to hunt in wide open places. And may Pack Rat's new home last for 40,000 years."

"Here, here," Javelina said.

The stories continued until it seemed everyone got their fill of treats, tea, sandwiches, and the cultivated life.

Then Deer Mother said, "It is time to return to the wild life, my friends."

She stood and pulled a small moonlight-colored bag from inside her glittery coat. Then she reached around the table and took cookies, small cupcakes, and colored ball candy and dropped them into the bag. Sister Laughs a Lot Mermaid and Ichika got up from the table and walked around to the Deer Mother.

"Thank you, all," Sister Laughs a Lot Mermaid said. "This was a lovely tea party."

The others nodded and said things like, "Of course," "any time," "our pleasure."

Deer Mother handed Ichika the bag filled with treats.

"Thank you, Deer Mother," Ichika said.

Deer Mother gently put her hand under Ichika's chin.

"You are welcome, dear one."

And then a cloud went over the Moon. Or someone snapped their fingers. The tea party was gone. In the next moment, Sister Laughs a Lot Mermaid and Ichika opened their eyes, and they were sitting on the bench near the fork in the dry river in the dark. The two looked at each other.

"It was all a dream?" Ichika asked.

Sister Laughs a Lot Mermaid shrugged. "A wonderful dream that we both had. We better get home before your mother worries."

Sister Laughs a Lot Mermaid stood and reached for Ichika's hand. The girl held up the bag Deer Mother had given her. It was still full of treats.

"It was not a dream," Ichika said. She grabbed Sister Laughs a Lot Mermaid's hand with her other hand, and they hurried home, running when they could see well enough, walking quickly when they couldn't, laughing and remembering the tea party.

When they got to the Old Mermaids Sanctuary and the house, Ichika dropped Sister Laughs a Lot Mermaid's hand and ran through the door into the lighted house.

"Momma!" Ichika cried. "I have brought you magic."

Sister Laughs a Lot Mermaid followed the child into the house. All the sister mermaids were crowded around Gimena. They moved out of the way to make room for the running child, and Sister Laughs a Lot Mermaid could see a man sitting next to Gimena.

"Poppa!" Ichika cried as she jumped into her father's lap, still holding tightly to the bag. Her father wrapped his arms around his daughter and held her tightly.

"We brought treats from the Deer Mother's tea party," Ichika said. She held the bag out to Grand Mother Yemaya Mermaid.

"Wonderful," Grand Mother said.

"Let me tell you about the tea party," Ichika said. "You wouldn't believe it. Except for right now seeing Poppa, it was the most wonderful thing I've ever seen."

Ichika told her parents and the Old Ems about their night while Sister Ruby Rosarita Mermaid and Sister Sheila Na Giggles Mermaid brought them tea. They all ate treats from the moonlight bag which stayed full until Ichika finished her story and they had all had their fill.

If the Shoe Fits: A Myla Alvarez Story

"**I** can't be certain, but I believe these are the shoes the Old Mermaids made for Mother Star Stupendous Mermaid. Remember when the Old Mermaids first came ashore on this new desert they didn't have shoes. They didn't know anything about shoes. But the desert is a prickly place and they needed protection for their tenderfeet. They eventually found someone near the Old Mermaids Sanctuary who made shoes, Mamma Josepha and Son Josephe.

"They did a fine job making pairs of shoes for each of the Old Mermaids. Except Mother Star Stupendous. Her feet hurt all the time. She didn't complain about it, but all the Old Mermaids could see that she was in pain from the blisters on her feet. The Old Mermaids sought out the Old Man and the Old Woman of the Mountains, and they suggested they talk with Betty, the Woman Who Weaves. So they did.

"Betty suggested that they go with the weavers for their annual trek into the desert to Spider Woman's Web. They gather spider webbing which they used to weave cloth. The Old Mermaids chose Sister DeeDee Lightful and Sissy Maggie Mermaid to go with the weavers, primarily because Sister DeeDee Lightful Mermaid was appropriately cautious and Sissy Maggie Mermaid was appropriately creative. The two Old Mermaids walked through the desert all night with Betty, the Woman Who Weaves, and the other weavers. At dawn, Betty told them they had reached Spider Woman's Enclave.

"The sun rose above the horizon and spread across the desert and lit up spider webbing on the jumping chollas, the teddy bear chollas, and all the prickly pears and other chollas. It looked as though the entire desert was held together by this golden webbing. The weavers brought out rattles, and they sang and rattled as the sun rose higher.

"They asked Old Grandmother Spider Woman for permission to use her thread. They promised to cherish it and use it for the good of all. They each whispered what they wished to use the thread for. Sister DeeDee Lightful Mermaid and Sissy Maggie Mermaid said they wanted to soothe Mother Star Stupendous Mermaid's aching soles. One of the weavers had her spinning wheel set up there and she began spinning the thread into balls. I'm not really sure how she did it, but each ball of thread was a different color.

"Betty told the Old Mermaids that every year one of the weavers became Old Grandmother Spider Woman for the day. At the end of the day, the weavers and the Old Mermaids feasted. Then they walked through the night until they reached home. Once they arrived at the Old Mermaids Sanctuary, Betty, the Woman Who Weaves, handed the Old Mermaids a ball of thread the color of the rainbow. Then she left with the other weavers.

"The Old Mermaids took the thread to Mamma Josepha and Son Josephe and asked them to use the thread to make a pair of shoes for Mother Star Stupendous Mermaid. At the end of thirteen days, Mamma Josepha presented the Old Mermaids with a pair of shoes that looked very much like these—maybe it was this exact same pair. I think so, but I can't be certain.

"The Old Mermaids took the shoes and the thread and they sewed sea stars into the shoes. Grand Mother Yemaya Mermaid began the orange spiral right here on the toes and Sister Laughs A Lot Mermaid finished it. Then the Old Mermaids gave the shoes to Mother Star Stupendous Mermaid. She put the shoes on, one at a time. Then she stood there in the Old Mermaids Sanctuary, her feet on the ground, and her eyes welled with tears.

"She said, 'I can feel the Old Sea between my toes. I can feel the sea fronds tickling my soles. And I can feel the sand of this old wash between my toes, too. I feel quite at home and my feet are very comfortable.'

"The Old Mermaids clapped and cheered. From then on Mother Star Stupendous Mermaid was rarely without her shoes, although she did lend them out on occasion if someone was feeling blue or not quite themselves—if their soles needed tickling. The story goes that the shoes fit anyone and everyone who tried them on and it only took a few minutes before the wearer felt like their old selves again. They say the shoes still have that effect on anyone who wears them to this day."

Grand Mother Yemaya Mermaid and the Old Sea

When the Old Sea first dried up and the Old Mermaids washed ashore in the New Desert, they weren't quite certain what had happened. Perhaps they had gotten some hint beforehand that all was not well in their world, but they didn't understand what they could or could not do to prevent it or stop it once it started. They got no chance to say goodbye to friends, family, or any of the creatures of the deep dark Old Sea. The Old Mermaids were all that was left of the Old Sea for as far as any of them could tell. Grand Mother Yemaya Mermaid felt it was her obligation and duty to find a way home. But she could not see or hear the Old Sea; she could only feel it in her bones. And so the Old Mermaids stepped out of the wash, left their past behind, and built the Old Mermaids Sanctuary.

Some of the Old Mermaids had a more difficult time adjusting than others. Grand Mother Yemaya Mermaid did not always know how to counsel them, but she did the best she could. She had known all there was to know about the Old Sea, but here, what did she know of unrelenting sun and blue skies? What did she know of dirt and rattlesnakes, trees with spikes, and howling coyotes?

Although most of the other Old Mermaids didn't realize it, Grand Mother Yemaya Mermaid was a bit out to sea for a while once they washed ashore on the New Desert. She still gave advice when asked, but she was not quite certain what her place was in this new world. After all, in the Old Sea she was thought of as the great goddess who birthed everything. She rose up out of the water on full moon nights, huge, dark, and powerful, her two tails reflecting the moon in her blue-green flashing scales. Here she felt heavy: weighted down by . . . everything.

One night she went out and stood with Mother Star Stupendous Mermaid as she stared up at the stars.

"The stars here are just lovely," Mother Star Stupendous Mermaid said.

"As lovely as they were in the Old Sea?" Grand Mother Yemaya Mermaid asked.

Mother Star Stupendous Mermaid laughed. "Of course. They are the same stars."

"I keep wondering what went wrong," Grand Mother Yemaya Mermaid said. "And I keep wondering why. But mostly, I cannot find the magic of this place. I miss all the wisdom of the Old Sea."

"I'm so sorry," Mother Star Stupendous Mermaid said. "I can see that it is difficult for you. I'm afraid my head has always been in the stars, so it's not that much different here for me, I suppose. But you are the deep blue sea. How lonesome it must get for you."

Grand Mother Yemaya Mermaid said, "I feel a longing for home that I've never had before."

"I do feel more awake here," Mother Star Stupendous Mermaid said. "Don't you? It's almost as if I were asleep before. And now I am awake. I have to pay attention to everything. It can be exhausting, it's true. But I love being awake."

Grand Mother Yemaya Mermaid pressed her lips together and thought about this. She supposed Mother Star Stupendous Mermaid was right. One had to be awake here: Injury and death lurked everywhere.

"I sometimes return to the Old Sea in my dreams," Mother Star Stupendous Mermaid said. "You were always the best dreamer. Perhaps you can go for a visit in your dreams."

That night, Grand Mother Yemaya Mermaid set her

intention to visit the Old Sea in her dreams. At first she had trouble falling asleep, but finally she was off to slumber land. Sure enough, she landed in the Old Sea. Once she got her bearings and her sea tails, she dove down deep into the water, going down, down, down until she reached a great green light, and then she swam past it until she found her mother, grand mother, great grandmother, and all the great Old Sea Goddesses. They swam together for a long while until they broke through the surface of the water to lounge on some rocks protruding from the Old Sea. The Oldest of Old Ems said to Grand Mother Yemaya Mermaid, "You may ask us anything."

Grand Mother Yemaya Mermaid thought about it for a bit, and then she said, "Why has this happened to us? Why must we suffer this fate?"

The Oldest of Old Mermaids said, "We don't know."

Grand Mother Yemaya Mermaid sat stunned for a moment. How could a goddess not know the answer to this simplest of questions?

"Know this, daughter," said one of the Oldest of Old Mermaids, "you hold the Old Sea and all the wisdom of the Old Sea in you. And all the wisdom of the New Desert, too."

"Laugh or weep," one of them said, "remember that we are in your tears."

Grand Mother Yemaya Mermaid nodded. And then she stood—she had legs again—and she walked away

                                    Kim Antieau

from the Oldest of the Old Mermaids and the Old Sea. She looked back once but spotted only seals on the rocks. Then she opened her eyes, and she was back in the Old Mermaids Sanctuary—sleeping on soaking wet sheets!

Sister DeeDee Lightful Mermaid and Sister Magdelene Mermaid were standing at the end of her bed. Sissy Maggie held a bucket as she was trying to catch the water from the bed.

"You cried in your sleep all night long," Sissy Maggie said, "and made lots of water."

"And your legs flashed as though they were tails again!" Sister DeeDee Lightful Mermaid said.

Grand Mother Yemaya Mermaid nodded as she got out of bed, soaking wet. The room smelled of the Old Sea. Grand Mother Yemaya Mermaid pulled off her nightgown and took the bucket from Sissy Maggie. She held her nightgown over the bucket and squeezed the water out of it. When she was finished with that, she pulled off the sheets, twisted them, and watched the water drip into the bucket. Then she dressed, grabbed some cloth from a storage closet, along with needle, thread, and scissors. She took all of that and the bucket of dream water, and she went out into the desert.

Once she found a big flat rock near the wash, Grand Mother Yemaya Mermaid sat down and began to sew. She cut 13 long rectangular pieces of cloth from the various scraps she had grabbed from the closet. Then she took the ball of thread and dropped it into the dirt. "May this thread be imbued with the power, healing, wonder, wisdom, and mystery of the New Desert," she said. Then she dropped the ball of thread into the bucket of her tears. "May this thread be imbued with all the power, healing, wonder, wisdom, and mystery of the Old Sea."

After a bit, Grand Mother Yemaya Mermaid threaded the needle with the now-magical thread. She began to sew, turning the cloth into 13 scarves, one for each Old Mermaid. As she pulled the needle through the cloth, she sang and whispered sea chanties and coyote howls and owl questions and hummingbird hums and waves rolling on sand into the cloth, along with the mysteries of the Old Sea and the New Desert. As the day wore on and became night and day and time stood still and carried on, Grand Mother Yemaya Mermaid sewed magic into the cloth. The more she sewed and the more she sang, the more she felt like herself again. She was no longer adrift.

Soon the other Old Mermaids came and sat with Grand Mother Yemaya Mermaid as she sewed and sang. They brought food and drink; they brought stories and songs. When she finished one scarf, she would drape it over an Old Mermaid and say something like, "Sister DeeDee Lightful Mermaid, I sewed into this scarf the mysteries and wisdom of the Old Sea and the New

Desert. And the Oldest of Old Mermaids wants you to know that laugh or weep, they swim in your tears."

One by one, the Old Mermaids had scarves with mysteries and wisdom sewn into them, until only one scarf was left. When Grand Mother Yemaya Mermaid finished that one, she placed it across her own shoulders and said, "Laugh or weep, they swim in our tears." And then Grand Mother Yemaya Mermaid looked around at the Old Mermaids, at the rocks, the empty wash, the blue blue sky. She listened and was quite certain she heard the Old Sea, if only for a moment, and then the pulsing stillness of the New Desert. She nodded. At least for now in this moment, all was right with her world.

Teas Galore at the Tea Shell

Beautiful as Sunset Tea

Will Find a Job Soon Tea

Roar of the Lion Tea

Essence of Coyote Laughter Tea

A Sip of Rattlesnake Moxie Tea

Crackle of Thunder Tea

Desert Faery Tea

Cloud Dust and Sliver of Moonlight Teas

Cloud Wanderer Tea

Hint of the Old Sea Tea

You're So Beautiful Tea

Wisdom of the Desert Faery Tea

Dances With Joy Tea

Laugh Yourself Silly Tea Day

Love the One You're Always With Tea Day

Hint of Winter Tea

Pretend Life is Great Tea

Old Mermaid Tears Tea

Found in
Translation

A young woman stumbled onto the Old Mermaids Sanctuary the other day. She was lost. She was more lost than any being I had ever seen, and remember, we walked out of the Old Sea and into the New Desert. We know about being lost.

She had thorns in her feet. They had gone right through her shoes. She had thorns in her arms. She had palo verde leaves in her hair. And her fingers were bleeding. She was wild-looking. Not good wild. Not natural wild. Lost human being wild.

We took out her thorns and helped her bathe her cuts and bruises. Sister Ruby Rosarita Mermaid made her soup. Sister Sheila Na Giggles Mermaid made her tea. Sissy Maggie Mermaid gave her clothes. She ate the soup, drank the tea, and put on the clothes. And she talked. She talked about all that had happened to her, she talked about all the misery she had seen, she talked about trying to get away from the roar that followed her everywhere.

"I can't stand it!" she finally said.

We listened and dried her tears.

Then Mother Star Stupendous Mermaid took the woman into the desert. They didn't walk far. Just far enough.

"Now be still," Mother Star Stupendous Mermaid said.

"But then all I will hear is the roar," she said.

"Then listen to it," Mother Star Stupendous Mermaid said. "Stand it. But first, first, listen for the birds. Listen to the cactus breathing. Listen to the sound of the air on the wings of the crow as she flies over. Listen to the trees."

Mother Star Stupendous Mermaid left the young woman. We glanced out at her a few times. We could tell she wanted to bolt, to run, to keep going, going, going. Gone. But she was learning what we all must learn: We can't run away from the roaring Inside.

When it became night in the desert, the young woman returned to us. "I am learning the language of my soul," she said. "The trees, birds, bees, wind, the coyotes and bobcats—they are all helping me with the translation."

We nodded. Mother Star Stupendous Mermaid said, "Yes, that is the way to be."

Later, we all went out into the desert night and held hands with the stars.

Ahhhhh.

Upon Reflection

Clouds spread across the sky like a huge old cottony comforter. You know the kind: It's old and the batting is scrunched up here and squeezed up there. And you're just about to throw it out or cut it up for scraps and then you remember when you made it or the time Sister Lyra Musica Mermaid threw it over Sister Laughs A Lot Mermaid when she couldn't even muster a smile. Or you put it up to your nose and you sense more than actually smell the sweet scent of Oliver the Old Cat who used to wander the Old Mermaids Sanctuary with Sister Ursula Divine Mermaid.

That's what is was like at the Old Mermaids Sanctuary last night as the Old Mermaids looked up at the gray clouds just as the sun dropped into the Old Sea and splashed scarlet and pink and rose up onto those clouds. At least that's what the Old Mermaids thought at first as they oohed and ahhed over the spectacle before them. And then Mother Star Stupendous Mermaid looked down at the pool and saw the sunset reflected there and she said, "Ahh, look, Sister Mermaids. We're seeing these clouds through the rose-colored reflection of the sun."

The Old Mermaids clapped and laughed out loud. Old Neighbor Pope was watching the sunset with the Old Mermaids. She said, "I think the expression is 'looking at the world through rose-colored glasses.' And it's not a good thing."

"Why isn't it a good thing?" Sissy Maggie Mermaid asked. "The clouds were lovely all puffy and gray up there in the sky. And now they are even more spectacular through our rose-colored glasses."

Old Neighbor Pope made a noise. Sometimes she thought the Old Mermaids just did not get it. "It means that you're not seeing things as they truly are when you look at them through rose-colored glasses," she explained.

Grand Mother Yemaya Mermaid said, "That is an interesting observation, Old Neighbor. I imagine that both ways of looking at the clouds are truthful and real. They're just different."

"But the clouds are not really scarlet-colored," the Old Neighbor insisted.

"Really?" Grand Mother Yemaya Mermaid said. She

looked up at the clouds again. "I'm sorry you can't see the scarlet. It is really quite magnificent."

Sister Sophia Mermaid and Eriskegal

S ister Sophia Mermaid found a cave on her way down from visiting the Old Woman and Old Man of the Mountains one day. She wasn't sure if it was the wise thing to do, but she went inside the darkness, lit a candle, and continued walking.

She walked until she heard, "Who goes there?"

She took a few more steps and the narrow passageway opened up. A woman the color of the green slime that covered the cave walls (for some unknown reason) was bent over a cauldron in the middle of the cave. Fire licked the black sides.

"Who are you?" the green slime woman screamed.

"I am Sister Sophia Mermaid," she said.

"I didn't call you," the woman screamed. "Why are you here? Don't you know I will tear your head off?"

Sister Sophia Mermaid shrugged. "I've already lost my tails and my home and my world. Not sure losing my head would change anything."

The woman looked up at her. "I am Eriskegal, goddess of the Underworld. Don't you know me?"

"I do not," Sister Sophia Mermaid said, "but I would be glad to know you."

Eriskegal sat on a stone bench near the cauldron. She waved to another stone bench and Sister Sophia Mermaid sat on it.

"Is this the Underworld?" Sister Sophia Mermaid asked.

Eriskegal roared with laughter. "No. I'm not sure what this place is. I was wandering and ended up here."

"Perhaps you needed sanctuary," Sister Sophia Mermaid said.

"Me? The goddess of death and destruction? Why would I need sanctuary?"

"Maybe you are tired of your routine," Sister Sophia Mermaid said.

Eriskegal laughed. "I am tired of the morons who stumble into my realm. Not a one them understands what truth is. Not a one of them has their heads out of their asses."

"Sounds like they have more than one head and more than one ass."

Eriskegal chuckled. "They don't understand reality."

"Do you?"

Eriskegal stared at Sister Sophia Mermaid quietly for a moment. Then she sighed. "We are born, we live, we die. What more?"

"Everything in-between is what more."

"They don't realize how short it all is," Eriskegal said. "They live their short stupid lives while I am stuck in the Underworld where I have to deal with their foolishness."

"You help them discover the truth," Sister Sophia Mermaid said. "Don't you? Or maybe they visit your realm to show you the truth. Each of them may carry a gem of truth for you."

"I hadn't thought of it that way," Eriskegal said. "Perhaps I should not slay them so quickly in the future. I will listen to what they have to say first."

Sister Sophia Mermaid laughed.

"What is funny?" the mistress of death asked.

"Um, nothing. Except: You actually slay them?"

Eriskegal nodded. "I think it's all metaphor. You know, they descend to the Underworld without all of their trappings from the outer world so they can face their true selves—including their death. Then they can ascend into the world again and live their authentic lives. Blah, blah, blah."

"Do you know your true self?" Sister Sophia Mermaid asked.

"I think my true self is actually a beach bum," Eriskegal said. "Without a care in the world."

"It sounds like you need a vacation," Sister Sophia Mermaid said. "I think I know just the place."

"Is it a sunny beach?"

"It is sunny," Sister Sophia Mermaid said, "and it used to be an ocean, so I guess now it's all beach. It's called the Old Mermaids Sanctuary."

"It sounds like a place where you are all delusional," Eriskegal said.

Sister Sophia Mermaid laughed. "No, not at all. It's just that everyone needs a break from death and destruction now and again."

"All right," Eriskegal said. "I will take a vacay."

They began walking out of the cave.

"And no slaying for a while," Sister Sophia Mermaid said.

"Even if someone pisses me off?" Eriskegal asked.

"Even then."

Origin Story: Sara's Place

Juan, Sara, and the girls walked into the sanctuary as if it was their first time. Sara stood at the wooden gate and ran her fingers over the hand-carved sign hanging there: Welcome to the Old Mermaids Sanctuary. On the side of the gate was an old bell. Juan picked up Nita so that she could ring it. She laughed and slapped her hand against it. Then Emmy did the same thing. Sara opened the gate and walked through it.

Before them was a lush garden surrounded by the curved arches of the three portals. At the center of the garden was a fountain. Two mermaids swam up out of the middle of the fountain. Their tails were entwined and they held hands. Water poured out of their hands.

They walked up to the wide portals. Chairs and tables were scattered here and there, near to the many doors that opened out onto the portal. Nita and Emmy ran through the main entrance and into the house. Sara and Juan followed them into the kitchen where Micaela was cooking. Micaela came and kissed them all. She smiled and clapped her hands. She was a different woman than the one Sara had met when she first came to the hacienda. She seemed younger, more alive. And she was boss of the kitchen. She told everyone to sit down and she would feed them.

Soon the smell of food brought people from all over the house and sanctuary into the kitchen. They sat at the long table in the kitchen and the tables outside. They laughed and talked and ate.

Everyone agreed that the main house at the Old Mermaids Sanctuary was alive. It seemed to have grown up out of the earth, and then the sun and stars came inside and gave it light and color. In the kitchen, flowers and vegetables grew as paintings on the tiled walls. Renaud said he had painted some of them, along with his love Lenardo, but he swore some of them had grown on their own. The household plates were made by Seraphina and her husband Roberto. Each was its own design. They had let Nita and Emmy help them paint them. Some had flowers on them. Others had pictures of seashells. A few had mermaids. Many of them had jackrabbits and coyotes on them. Some of them were filled with colorful designs.

                                    Kim Antieau

Those were the plates everyone ate off of that first day at the Old Mermaids Sanctuary. It wasn't actually the first day, but it felt like it because Sara and the girls were not going back to the hacienda. And that night, Nita and Emmy slept in their room—the room they had helped paint. Their handprints went all around the bottom of the room. When Renaud had asked them what animals they wanted painted on their walls, they both cried, "Jack the Rabbit!" And so he had painted giant jackrabbits all over the walls, except right above the hand prints. There he had painted Old Mermaids swimming across the walls. He said he had painted four, one for each wall, yet over night they had multiplied into thirteen.

Sara had lined the shelves in the girls' room with books, especially books filled with faery tales. Before they went to sleep that first night, they each said goodnight to the jackrabbits, the coyotes, the eagles, the auld sea, the auld mother, Papa Javier and Papa Juan and all the good folk, visible and invisible.

Sara kissed them goodnight and then left the room. She stood looking at their closed blue door. On it hung a little wooden sign that read "Emmy & Juanita's Room." The girls had written their names themselves. Sara wondered if other two and half year olds could do that.

People started coming to the sanctuary almost as soon as Sara and the girls made it their home. Some people came to look at the beauty of it. To marvel at the mermaid fountain: no one was quite sure where the water came from or how it flowed through the mermaids, not even the man who built it. Sara wondered if they had somehow tapped into the spring Murphy had said was near the mermaid wall. Sara had never found it.

She did hear the singing. Many people did. It was only on particular nights or particular days. When it was really cold or hot. Or when the sun was down or the sun was up. When the moon was dark or the moon was full. They all heard the mermaids singing. And they all agreed they weren't trying to lure them away from anything or to anything. It was a welcome home song.

Some people came to help Sara with the sewing. Weavers came too. They made their own yarn at the Old Mermaids Sanctuary. And they made clothes. Quilts and blankets too. They sold them to those who could pay for them and gave the rest away. Some women left their husbands and came to the sanctuary and sewed.

Others helped in the garden. Or in the kitchen. No man ever followed their wives into the Old Mermaids Sanctuary. A few came to the gate, but they never went through it if they were angry. Some heard the mermaids singing, and they sat down and wept.

A few potters lived at the sanctuary for a time. Artists

of all kinds came. They carved and painted and left gifts around the sanctuary. Musicians played outside under the moon.

Animals of all kinds visited the sanctuary, and Sara asked that no one harm any of them. Horses began showing up, too, and Juan took care of them. Some stayed to be with the people, others moved on, like other visitors.

Renaud and Leonardi moved into the sanctuary. The Englishman had left the ranch and sold it to Gabriel, who ran it much the way the Englishman did, except he had more fun and the food was better. Madeleine came and went.

The girls grew and flourished in the sanctuary. They collected rocks and seashells. They found seashells in the wash every spring after the river dried up. No one understood where the shells had come from, but everyone agreed they must be a gift from the auld ma and the auld sea for her dearest children.

Sister Ruby Rosarita Mermaid and the Sous Chef

From the Visitor's Log at the Old Mermaids Sanctuary:

This might be longer than your average comment on your log, my dear Old Mermaids, but I hope you'll add it anyway. Or keep it just for you. It doesn't matter. I want to say some things. Yes, my time at the Sanctuary was wonderful, as so many of your previous guests wrote in the log. (I read it before I left.) The conversations were funny and profound—and sometimes difficult to follow if Sister Sophia Mermaid and Sister Magdelene Mermaid began going down one obscure path or another, as so many other guests have mentioned. And the food was divine.

But I have more to say. I came to the Sanctuary with a particular goal in mind. I wanted a profound spiritual experience. I wanted the gates of amazing revelations to open and let me in. I wanted to be suddenly changed so that I had endless patience, was kind to everyone I met, and was wildly successful at everything I did. I came here so tired of struggling. I came here so tired, period.

You all asked me to help out Sister Ruby Rosarita Mermaid because of the fall celebrations. The days and nights had gotten a bit cooler, and it was harvest time. The whole community was coming to the Sanctuary for days of feasting, singing, dancing, and having a good time.

I was surprised when you asked me to help cook. I thought I would be sent to a mountaintop to contemplate the heavens, maybe with Mother Star Stupendous Mermaid at my side. Or maybe I would walk the wash with Grand Mother Yemaya Mermaid whilst gazing at the navel of the Universe. Or match wits with Sister Sophia Mermaid. I had hoped to learn the best spells and chants from Sisters Bridget and Faye Mermaid. But no. I was to help Sister Ruby Rosarita Mermaid cook.

Cook. Good grief. That was what I had to do in my parents' house. That was what I had to do in my own life, to keep myself fed. But it was . . . meaningless. Cooking. It was just one of those trivial tasks we have to do every day. I was certain I couldn't learn anything while cook-

                                   Kim Antieau

ing at the Sanctuary. I didn't believe I could alleviate my suffering by cooking or serving others what we had cooked. But I was willing to give it a try.

It didn't start out well. I was resentful. I expected more. I had come here full of high hopes. Instead, I experienced nothing out of the ordinary.

Even the sisters were disappointing. I know, I know. I thought every word out of their mouths would be perfect. Inspiring. Absolutely revelatory. It wasn't. They were passionate about some things, depending upon the sister. They got angry. They got sad. They were happy. Sometimes they were ecstatic. I thought, how could I learn from them if they aren't always patient, if they get angry? They are no better than me.

I helped Sister Ruby Rosarita Mermaid with the cooking. Before we started one morning, she ran a piece of cloth under the water, wrung it out, and then put it around her neck.

"Ahhhh," she said. "Much better. Would you like one, too?"

"What for?" I asked.

"To help with the heat," she said. She was wearing a long cotton skirt the color of pomegranate along with a peach-colored shirt. She had a droopy flower in her hair. I kept wondering what kind of flower could it possibly be in a place that was so desolate, hot, and flowerless.

She was claiming a wet cloth around the neck helped

with the heat? That sounded impossible and stupid to me. I said, "No. I don't think so. I'm surprised you have to use it. I thought all the Old Mermaids were naturally acclimated to the heat."

Sister Ruby Rosarita Mermaid laughed. "Not exactly. Some of us are a little more comfortable in the heat than others. But this kitchen gets very hot." She tapped the cloth hanging around her neck. "And this is a touch of magic that helps me through the day."

We boiled beans that first day, if I remember correctly. Sister Ruby Rosarita Mermaid kept singing, "Beans, beans, we're mermaid queens. Make yourself the best we've ever seen."

She said to me, "As every wise woman everywhere knows, you always talk to the food, just as you always talk to the plants the food comes from."

She had a little poem or song for every part of the process. And she delighted in it all. Except when she didn't. She complained about the heat now and again, threatened to strip herself naked and cook that way, or find her way back to the Old Sea and jump in. I kept thinking if she were truly enlightened, if she were truly a wise person, she would not complain. She would not be hot. I was hot. I was miserable, but I was not an enlightened person.

She talked to her spoon, too. I am not joking. She would say things like, "Spoon, spoon, by this afternoon help us create a bean boon." Or rice boon. Vegetable boon. Whatever we were cooking. Her chants were always corny, always bad poetry.

She would laugh, sometimes kiss the spoon, and then dip it into whatever we were cooking after she sang.

She always had something cooking on the stove besides what we were making for the celebration, usually a pot of stew or soup she called the Never Too Many Cooks Soup or Stew. It started out with a pot of water. "From water we come, to water we return," Sister Ruby Rosarita Mermaid would say. She would glance over at me and shrug. "Once a mermaid, always a mermaid."

People were in and out of the kitchen all day. One day Old Neighbor Woman stopped by, tasted the water, and said, "Oh my. Delicious. But wouldn't it be even better with some of my carrots? They overwintered. And new onions. Some garlic." And so we would cut up those and drop them into the soup.

Sister Bridget Mermaid came by with some Old Mermaid tears. Someone—maybe Sister DeeDee Lightful Mermaid—added a few drops of the Old Mermaids Elixir.

Annie Who Loves Birds brought pieces of fish and dropped them into the pot. "All the correct prayers and blessings were sung," she said. As we stirred the pot when Annie left, I asked Sister Ruby Rosarita Mermaid, "What are the correct prayers?"

"Whatever you say from your heart," she answered. "The words aren't as important as the intent. At least that is true here. Isn't that true where you are from?"

I thought about it for a moment, and then I said, "I don't know. We don't generally talk to anyone but other human beings."

"Oh." That was all she said about that.

Throughout the day, people dropped things into the soup that became a stew and then a soup and then a stew and then who knows what. Sister Ruby Rosarita Mermaid would stir, let it cook, and then taste. "A touch of salt, maybe," she would say, "to give it that tang." Or maybe, "A bit of laughter." And then she would laugh like some kind of mad woman—or someone who was really happy. More than once, she asked me to taste the concoction and see what it needed. I finally said, "Closure." She laughed. "I agree," and she put the lid on the soup. "Come and get it as it is!" she called, and so people ate from the pot for the rest of the day.

Often we went out to the walled garden. Somehow she had made a little garden of Eden in the desert. When I asked her how, she said, "Oh, just a few ingredients in the right proportion. Like seeds, earth, water, sun. Have you ever looked at a seed, really? Have you ever thought about it?"

We were crouched near the ground picking lettuce or some other kind of greens. Shade from several pomegranate trees fell over us. I could smell dirt and something tangy or fruity. I couldn't quite place it. I balanced on one of my hands with my palm pressed against the kitty litter-like dirt. It was the first time since I had gotten there that I wasn't immediately worried that a scorpion or rattlesnake was going to sneak out of somewhere and get me.

"What about a seed?" I asked.

"Everything is in that seed," she said. "Everything is in it to become a tree, for instance. Or lettuce. Or a fig tree that grows figs. It has its own recipe. Right in that seed. It's miraculous. It's utter magic."

"That's just science," I said.

She nodded. "Of course. And magic. I once asked Sister Sophia Mermaid what the root meaning of magic was. You know, because words are like plants. They have roots, too." She grinned. Our basket was full so we stood and stayed in the shade for a few moments, talking. "She told me it meant harnessing natural forces to create marvels. That's science. It's about transformation. I mean, think about cooking. Wow. I was so fortunate that I discovered cooking when we came to the New Desert. Some of the other Old Mermaids had trouble adjusting. I never did. I had a purpose. I had to keep us nourished. The Old Neighbors—especially the Witch from Coyote Hill—helped me. In the Old Sea, we were magic. Us. Our bodies. Here we have to create magic or recognize it. We're different here. Everything is different. It's as if everything before we got to the New Desert was a dream, without consequence, and now we're here and everything is consequential. I mean, I can change my mind about something and everything suddenly changes. Or nothing changes except me. I'm in a constant state of transformation here. I watch it every day: I take ingredients, put them together, say a few words, and voila! we have a transformation. We've created a new thing. A new dish. I am a magician! Ta da!" She put her arm up into the air. "That is so amazing to me."

"Cooking seems so ordinary," I said to her. "We do it every day."

"Isn't that grand?" she asked. "We make magic constantly in this new world. I love that."

I had never thought about cooking like that before. I hadn't thought about anything like that before. I couldn't think about it any longer because it was time for the celebrations. We finished cooking the rice, beans, and putting together several casseroles. We set the food out by that strange pool. The neighbors all brought dishes, too. We had music, dancing, and tall tales, as well as food.

At some point I had to run back into the house for something, and I stopped on my way to the kitchen, noticing the murals on the walls. I had seen them before but I had thought of them as amateur attempts at art.

Now the mountains were familiar—yes, there was the north crevice and that copse of trees. Perfect. And the ocean scenes. Ahhh, the dolphins the sisters spoke about so fondly. The sea stars that reflected the night sky. I could almost hear the waves as I stared at the blue-green world. And the wash painted on the walls, barely discernible from the walls themselves. I felt something bubbling up inside me as I looked at it. I could feel the magic of it in my bones. How the wash transformed every year from something akin to a ditch into a creek and then a river and then back again. How powerful to cross those thresholds again and again—to be able to change like that was wondrous.

When I went into the kitchen, everything seemed to glow or pulse. As if it had all come alive during the minutes I had been outside. But no, that wasn't what happened. It hadn't changed: I had. I laughed as I stirred the soup. It smelled divine. Why had I thought it smelled like rotten cabbage? For a moment, I wondered which was true: Did it smell divine or like rotten cabbage? Could both be true? Yes! Maybe not rotten cabbage. Maybe divine cabbage. That idea made me giggle.

I grabbed the spoons Sister Ruby Rosarita Mermaid had asked me to get, and then I went back to the party. I wanted to hear the stories. I had a few of my own to tell.

Some days later, I left the Old Mermaids Sanctuary and returned home. Everything felt dull again. Then I remembered what Sister Ruby Rosarita Mermaid had done most mornings: She went outside and stood on the bare earth; she sang up the sun; she talked to plants in the garden, to the clouds in the sky, to the blue door; she sang chants to the dishes she prepared. I began doing the same, only I did it my way. And everything changed, except that which stayed the same.

I wanted to write this to you, I wanted to share all this, to tell you I understand magic now. I understand transformation. I see beauty. I see ugliness. I see situations that must be changed. I see things that need to stay the same. Sometimes I know what to do. Sometimes I do not. Sometimes I am angry. Sometimes I am sad. Often I am happy. More often I am filled with love and awe. Wow. Wow. Wow. I feel like a magician, a real live magic-maker.

Old Mermaids, thank you for teaching me to cook.

Bear Woman and Sister DeeDee Lightful Mermaid

After the Old Mermaids washed ashore on the New Desert, they had to quickly learn to survive. Although some were afraid, they didn't have much time for reflection or for many more tears. Their world had ended. All they had known was gone. They had each other—and the New Desert and the Old Neighbors.

With the help of the Old Neighbors, the Old Mermaids built their house, planted a garden, and established the Old Mermaids Sanctuary. It was a wonder to behold. Each Old Mermaid had her place in this new world.

Some of them stumbled now and again. After they all seemed to settle in, after they seemed to have accepted their fate, after nearly all of them adjusted to their new life, Sister DeeDee Lightful Mermaid realized she was not herself. She did not delight in anything.

This was such a new feeling for her that she didn't know what to do or what not to do. One day as she was walking in the desert beneath the seemingly unrelenting Sun, she heard a crow fly overhead. She heard the whoosh, whoosh, whoosh of the crow's wings in the dry air. She looked up and watched the bird fly toward Woman's Crying Summit. She decided to follow the bird.

She kept waiting for the crow to disappear from her view, but it didn't. Whenever she lagged behind, the crow would alight on something taller than either of them and wait for her. Eventually after an hour, a day, a week, a month, they were up the side of the mountain amongst pine trees. The crow perched on top of one and stayed there.

Sister DeeDee Lightful Mermaid stopped and looked around. Now what? Nothing happened. The Sun moved slowly across the sky. The crow groomed itself. Sister DeeDee Lightful Mermaid still did not feel like herself. She started to think about returning home. Then she heard a stirring in the leaves. She looked over and saw a Bear Woman standing not far from her. Or maybe it was a Bear. Or a Woman. She wasn't certain. Bears were new to her, although Sister Ursula Divine Mermaid had told her about a bear she had met on the mountains. Was this the same one?

"You have come to Bear Country," Bear Woman said. "Do you wish to die or know yourself better?"

"I want to feel better," Sister DeeDee Lightful Mermaid said.

"That was not one of the choices," Bear Woman said.

"I long for the Old Sea," Sister DeeDee Lightful Mermaid said.

Bear Woman nodded. "Of course. You miss the darkness. Come. I will lend you mine. It is not watery, but it is what I have."

Sister DeeDee Lightful Mermaid followed Bear Woman to a cave in the mountainside. Bear Woman pointed to the darkness. "Is this what you need?"

"In the darkness, I shine," Sister DeeDee Lightful Mermaid said. "In the light, I am invisible."

"And this bothers you?" Bear Woman asked.

"I suppose it does," Sister DeeDee Lightful Mermaid said.

"I will keep the others away," Bear Woman said. "The creatures of the night, as it were. But other monsters may reside within."

Sister DeeDee Lightful Mermaid nodded. She understood. She stepped into the darkness. When her eyes adjusted, she still saw nothing. She felt around until her hands found a giant bed in the middle of this cave of darkness. Sister DeeDee Lightful Mermaid climbed into the bed.

She sat for an hour, a day, a month, a year. She breathed in the darkness and breathed out the darkness. She was relieved to be away from the harsh light of the Sun.

At some point, she heard a kind of buzzing in the room or a whirring of tiny wings. She held her fingers out to the darkness and something landed on one of her fingers. It was so light she could barely feel the claws clutching her finger.

"Let there be light," she whispered. And suddenly the thing on her finger was illuminated, as though a multi-colored flame had been lit from within. A blue-green hummingbird was perched on her finger and now watched her intently. It was one of the most beautiful sights Sister DeeDee Lightful Mermaid had ever seen and she had seen much beauty in her life. Joy surged through her body.

Then she heard—from the bird?—"Let there be light." She looked down, and she was glowing from within, too. She smiled.

"I am myself again," she said.

The hummingbird flew away. Sister DeeDee Lightful Mermaid followed it out of the cave and into the sun-shine. Bear Woman and the crow were gone, but the day was young. She could get home before dinner. She hurried down the slope of the mountain.

I won't say Sister DeeDee Lightful Mermaid never had any trouble again, because she did now and again, but gradually she began to feel at home in her body and in the New Desert. And when she didn't, she found darkness to wrap around her.

Sister Laughs A Lot Mermaid and the Old Turkeys

Sister Laughs A Lot Mermaid was the first Old Em to stumble upon the wild turkeys. When she first saw them, she thought they were giants, at least giants as far as birds go. They were in a group under several Old Sycamore trees. Each turkey person was dressed in dark colorful clothes. Or feathers. Sister Laughs A Lot Mermaid couldn't tell which. She laughed and clapped her hands and was ready for adventure.

A big Ole Turkey Tom walked up to the Old Em. He puffed up his feathers at her.

"Would you care to walk on the wild side with me?" he asked, spreading his tail feathers up and behind him. He sure was pretty.

"What exactly would that entail?" she asked.

Ole Turkey Tom laughed. "I get it," he said. "That's funny as hell. En-tail. My tail is swell."

"Your tail is swell?"

"I need to tell the others."

Soon the Turkey People had gathered around her. They took turns telling jokes and puffing out their tails. Sister Laughs A Lot Mermaid did not always understand their jokes, but she laughed anyway. Jenny Wild Turkey kept saying to the males, "Stop doing that. She's an Old Em. She's not interested in your bones or feathers."

Ole Turkey Tom invited all the Old Mermaids for a feast under the sycamores. Sister Laughs A Lot Mermaid accepted on their behalf and ran back to camp to tell the Old Ems.

The Old Mermaids spent some time trying to figure out what to bring to the feast.

"Are they people or turkeys?" Sister Sophia Mermaid asked. "Are they faery and flighty? It's difficult to know."

They had brought nuts with them on their trip to the canyon, so they decided they would offer nuts. They dressed in whatever finery they had and soon walked to where the Old Wild Turkeys were awaiting them.

The Old Ems walked into the sycamore woods and were amazed to see a long table laden with food awaiting them. Sister Laughs A Lot Mermaid couldn't tell right away what the food was because Ole Tom Turkey and the others gathered around them. The Turkey Women put feathers in the Old Ems' hair, and the Turkey Men puffed out their chests and fanned their tail feathers.

Grand Mother Yemaya Mermaid held out their bowl of various nuts. "We hope this is enough for your splendid feast."

Ole Tom Turkey took the bowl and put it on the table.

"Thank you," Ole Tom Turkey said. "We appreciate it, but we have plenty. For our main dish, we always carve up a little mermaid."

"You carve up a little mermaid?" Sister Laughs A Lot Mermaid asked, momentarily alarmed.

Ole Tom Turkey laughed. "We always serve up a little lemonade." He slapped Sister Laughs A Lot Mermaid on the back. "You are a funny Old Mermaid."

"So I've been told," she said.

"You are very old?" he asked.

Jenny Wild Turkey opened her arms and said, "Let us break bread before this old turkey tries to make another joke."

And so they feasted on nuts and fruits and seeds and cakes. They all told jokes, and half of them the Old Mermaids didn't understand. It didn't matter. A good time was had by all, and Sister Laughs A Lot Mermaid made sure no little or big mermaids were hurt in the making of the feast.

Origin Story: Old Mermaids Chapel

One day Juan said to Sara, "This is a sanctuary," he said, "and I think a sanctuary needs a church. A church of the Old Mermaids." He pointed up the path where the old mermaid wall was. "I think we should build it right there and make the wall part of it. And we'll paint the inside and fill it with old mermaids and the old sea."

Sara smiled at him. "You're doing this because you think I'm unhappy," she said. "I'm not. I'm sometimes sad for the sea and my ma."

He kissed her forehead. "Can I build it for you?"

She nodded. "You can."

And he did. It was a tiny church. As round as can be, built mostly from stone. As far as Sara could tell, every-one from the sanctuary and everyone else they knew came and helped. Everyone of them went into the chapel and painted something: mermaids, seashells, fish, trees, lions, bears, coyotes, little girls with fish tails and wings on their hearts. And the old mermaid wall was part of it all. Juan left off the ceiling so that it was exposed to all the elements they loved. The chapel looked as though it was already falling into ruins.

When Sara stepped into it for the first time after they finished, she could hear the roar of the Old Sea.

"It's as if I'm inside a seashell," she whispered to Juan. "You did this? It's beautiful. I may never leave." She kissed him.

That night she slept in the tiny church of the old mermaids. In the morning, she heard the mermaids whispering to her. She got up and went outside. She followed the sound into the desert until she saw a spot of green. She went to it and discovered a tiny spring bubbling up from the earth. She smiled and bent over it.

Recipe for Success

Sister Sophia Mermaid sometimes tells people, "The best recipe for success is to let go of pre-conceived ideas about everything. Then the path to the truth will show itself to you. It's not always pleasant, but it's better to make choices and decisions based on reality." I should point out that the Old Mermaids' definition of success has nothing to do with money. It is about prosperity of the soul. For them, this means having good relations with the land and all the critters (human and otherwise)—and with the Cosmos in general.

Sister Bea Wilder Mermaid and the Owl

One full Moon evening, Sister Bea Wilder Mermaid set off in the wash in search of jackrabbits dancing in the light of the full Moon. She had heard from the Old Neighbors that the jackrabbits do this regularly, even though Sister Bea had not found anyone who had actually witnessed it. She didn't really think she would find the jackrabbits dancing in the moonlight, but she hadn't been feeling herself lately. She couldn't figure out who she was in this new world and how she fit into the routine of every day life. She did not feel at home today or most days.

It was a little chilly since it was winter, so she had bundled up in a bright red coat Sissy Maggie had made for her. She wore a hat, scarf, and gloves that Sister DeeDee Lightful Mermaid had knit for her. Those had lots of holes in them, left by Sister DeeDee Lightful so that the "light could get in here and there."

The full Moon light was so bright that it was nearly as light out as daylight only so vastly different that Sister Bea Wilder Mermaid couldn't think of the words to describe the difference even to herself. Walking in the moonlight was like walking in a dream, only brighter and more real, she supposed, now that she had started dreaming.

Suddenly a shadow fell across her, and Sister Bea Wilder Mermaid looked up just in time to see a great horned owl fly overhead. She hadn't heard the bird's wings flap because the owl's wings were silent. The owl landed in the Y of a snag of a long dead mesquite tree and stared at Sister Bea Wilder Mermaid who stopped walking and stared right back.

The owl's eyes shined in the moonlight like two perfect silver coins.

It hooted, "Who, who?"

Sister Bea Wilder Mermaid nodded and said, "Are you asking yourself or are you asking me? Because if you're asking me who I am, I am Sister Bea Wilder Mermaid. At your service. If you're really asking who I am deep down, I guess I don't know. Although why would an owl ask me about my deepest truths? I don't actually think I have a deeper truth. I just am what I am. How about you? Who are you? Who?"

The owl blinked. And then it said, "I hadn't thought about it before. I was just trying to start a conversation."

"You succeeded," Sister Bea Wilder Mermaid said.

"With another owl," it said. "I wanted to start a conversation with another owl."

"Ahhh," Sister Bea Wilder Mermaid said. "I am not an owl. At least, not yet. Do you want to give me any hints on how to become one?"

"Again," the owl said, "I really haven't given this much thought. But perhaps asking the same insistent question over and over is a start. Wait. I hear someone calling out that question in the distance. Who, who, what a hoot. It might be my one true love."

Sister Bea Wilder Mermaid laughed. "You weren't really trying to start a conversation. You were looking for love."

The owl shrugged. "What is an identity crisis compared with love?"

It opened its giant wings and took off in the direction of the Moon or the sound of the owl's true love.

Sister Bea Wilder Mermaid stood quietly for a minute. What was an identity crisis compared to love? She sighed deeply. She loved being under this full Moon with her feet pressed firmly in the sand. She loved the owl. She loved the stars above. She loved their home and her sister mermaids. She grinned. She was starting to think like Sister Magdelene Mermaid.

She turned around and began running down the wash toward home. A bunny rabbit ran beside her, up out of the wash, for a while. Then a coyote replaced the rabbit. And then a stag. Along came a mountain lion. Then a bear. Sister Bea Wilder Mermaid laughed as she ran.

Just then she reached the house where Sister Ursula Divine Mermaid flung open the door and leaned out.

"There you are," Sister Laughs a Lot Mermaid said as she came to the door to stand next to Sister Ursula Divine Mermaid.

"We've been waiting for you," Sister Faye Mermaid said. "The wild times can't start without you."

"Who is it?" Grand Mother Yemaya Mermaid called from inside the house.

"It's me. Sister Bea Wilder Mermaid," she said. "I'm home."

Sister Ursula Divine Mermaid and Coyote Woman

The Old Mermaids adored the coyotes as much as any of the wildlife that made their home on the Sanctuary. Sister Ursula Divine Mermaid spent more of her time with coyotes than the other sisters, probably because often she wandered the desert alone, and coyote pups were curious about her. In fact, one day, they steered her to Coyote Mother who lived in a den that looked down on most of the Old Neighbors and the Old Mermaids Sanctuary. Coyote Mother called it a den, but it reminded Sister Ursula Divine Mermaid of some of the palaces in the Old Sea if she looked at it one way. If she looked at it another way, it looked like a shack in the desert.

Coyote Woman stood outside the Den with her hands on her hips with her long tongue hanging out like it was just too damn hot to keep it in. When Sister Ursula Divine Mermaid blinked, the coyote's tongue was gone and the woman was smiling, her yellow-green eyes lit up by the sun. Many small coyote children ran around her and the various cactuses around the Den, yipping, shouting, whimpering, throwing up dust.

"Hey, don't let your brother do that to you!" Coyote Woman said. "Beat the crap out of him next time. Yes, like that. Good. I'll give you something to whimper about if you bite your sister again. You, too much dust, you'll be sneezing all night."

Coyote Woman looked over at Sister Ursula Divine Mermaid. "It's a wild life, ain't it?"

"I suppose."

"The kiddos say you are very serious as you walk around in the desert," Coyote Woman said. "In the summer. They think you might be loco. And not in the good way. Whatcha need? A good story? A run through the desert?"

"A run through the desert sounds good," Sister Ursula Divine Mermaid said.

"You are loco!" Coyote Woman said. "That sun could fry the scales off you in two seconds flat."

"I don't have scales," Sister Ursula Divine Mermaid said. "Any more."

                                   Kim Antieau

Coyote Woman laughed. "Sure you do. Just like I have claws."

"Sometimes it is too dry and too hot here and I wish it were different."

"If wishes were rabbits, I'd be a lot fatter," Coyote Woman said. "This won't last forever. So come on in and tell me some tall tales."

Sister Bridget Mermaid Sends Blessings

May the power of the Old Sea be on you.

May the power of the New Desert be on you.

May the mysteries of the Old Sea on you.

May the magic of the New Desert be on you.

May the beauty of the cactus blooms be on you.

May the strength of the saguaros be on you.

May you know peace.

May you know good health.

May you know love.

May you know prosperity all the days of your life.

Kim Antieau

Sister Sophia Mermaid and the Javelina

One evening Sister Sophia Mermaid was walking down a smaller wash by the Old Mermaids Sanctuary. They called it Rabbit Run because it sometimes seemed full of rabbits. Not full like it was during the summer rains when every puddle became an ocean and every wash or scrape in the dirt became a river. Still, they saw many rabbits there and other creatures, too. On this particular day, Sister Sophia Mermaid was surprised to see a lone javelina coming toward her down the wash.

The Old Mermaid stopped because she knew javelinas didn't see particularly well, and they were built like moving brick walls: She did not want it to run into her. Of course, many of the washes around the Old Mermaids Sanctuary were entryways from here to there, so this javelina could have been a faery creature. She saw no bowtie, no hat, tiny high heels, or anything like that which would tell her it was a faery peccary.

But then it stopped a few feet from her, sat on its haunches, and sighed. It looked at her with big blue eyes. She had never seen a javelina with blue eyes.

"Does something ail ye, friend?" Sister Sophia Mermaid asked.

"I've left the herd to find another way," it said. "But it is exhausting."

"Why did you want to find another way?" Sister Sophia Mermaid asked. "Was something wrong with the old way?"

"They're always together," it said. "And when I disagreed with them about anything, they threatened to throw me out."

"Ahhh," she said. "So you were asked to leave?"

"You could put it that way," it said. "They are always rubbing up against each other. We've always got to protect the babies. We're looking for food or sleeping all the time."

Sister Sophia Mermaid laughed. "Isn't that just life?"

"I want something more," it said.

"Are you sure you're a javelina?" Sister Sophia Mermaid asked. "You talk and you have blue eyes."

"Are you sure you're an Old Mermaid?" it asked. "You talk to me and you have no tails."

"I suppose you have a point," Sister Sophia Mermaid said. "I only thought maybe you are part faery. A javelina faery foundling. I've never heard of such a thing, but it might exist."

"Look, I just want to know if you've seen my herd," it said. "I'm ready to go home."

"But if they kicked you out, can you go back?" Sister Sophia Mermaid asked.

"I will try to fit in better," it said. "I'll pretend to like it when we get in a group and rub each other. I won't argue so much."

Sister Sophia Mermaid shook her head. "That sounds a lot like the humans I know."

"I tried being by myself, but ya know, there's not a lot of options for people like me in the world. I mean, what else am I gonna do? A javelina is a javelina is a javelina."

"I was once an Old Sea Old Mermaid," Sister Sophia Mermaid said. "Look at me now." She did a little dance on her two feet. "And I didn't have a choice."

"Apples and oranges," it said. "Besides, you're still you. You just left the Old Sea. From what I understand. I am not an expert on Old Mermaids. And you are not an expert on javelinas."

"You are so right," Sister Sophia Mermaid said. "I have no idea what you need or what you should do. I did see a lot of hoof prints not far from the Tea Shell this morning. And there are plenty of prickly pears for you to eat in that area. I bet you'd hear all kinds of great conversations from all kinds of flora and fauna there and you might run into your herd, too. I'll show you."

"Yes, that's what I want," it said. "Conversation. How many times a day can we talk about what we're going to eat next or how many times we'll rub musk on each other. Or then there's no talk, just snuffling. It's torturous."

"I can't promise no talk about eating," Sister Sophia Mermaid said, "but I'm guessing there won't be much snuffling, at least not until your herd passes by."

They began walking down the wash toward the Tea Shell.

"Thank you for listening and for not trying to solve me," it said. "Humans do have trouble listening to troubles, don't they?"

"I'm not human," Sister Sophia Mermaid said.

"You look pretty human to me," it said. "But I won't hold that against you."

"Thank you," she said. "You look pretty pig-like, but I won't hold that against you."

"Hey, I am not a pig," it said. "Please. Have some respect. I may have been kicked out of my herd, but I'm not a garbage-eater!"

"Of course not," she said. "You are a blue-eyed talking peccary who dines on splendid cactus fruit and has an identify crisis. I can relate."

"Your eyes do not look blue," it said. "So it must mean you like cactus fruit."

Sister Sophia Mermaid nodded.

"You've never had an identity crisis?" it asked. "Not even when you left the Old Sea?"

"I suppose I was confused at first," Sister Sophia Mermaid said. "I felt like I was being punished for something, but I didn't know what it was. It sometimes feels like that when bad things happen. But ya know, I was still me. A little know it all. A little crotchety."

"And they never kicked you out?"

"The other Old Ems? Oh no. We are not all the same. We welcome conversation and dissent."

"Can I become an Old Mermaid?" it asked. "I promise to argue with you on a regular basis."

Sister Sophia Mermaid laughed. "You are welcome to stay on the Sanctuary for as long as you like." She shrugged. "I bet you'll find your way here. Most creatures do. We're almost there."

"I hear voices," the javelina said excitedly. "I wonder what they're talking about. I bet it is something exciting."

"Well, it'll be something," she said. "There's always something."

And the peccary and Old Mermaid hurried toward the Tea Shell where many other Old Mermaids awaited them.

Sister Faye Mermaid and the Mysteries

Sister Faye Mermaid knew just about everything, except those things she didn't know. And when she didn't know, she relied on her ability to string words together in such a way that time stopped or time sped up or energy flowed or energy swirled and minds were changed and life was transformed. Or it wasn't. Sometimes magic worked. Sometimes it didn't. Or rather, sometimes the answer was yes and sometimes the answer was no. The Universe is a mysterious place.

When Sister Faye Mermaid first arrived on the shores of the New Desert, she was speechless. I don't mean she didn't talk. She wasn't mute. She had no enchantments to sing, no poems to soothe. She knew she had to listen to this new world before she could find the right words. For a while, she did not understand the world. The Old

Ems were accustomed to looking to Sister Faye Mermaid when they needed to change the way things were. Yet now, it seemed none of them could change anything.

Wisely, Sister Faye Mermaid began to observe her beloved Old Mermaids as they adjusted to the new world. She noticed how Sister Sheila Na Giggles Mermaid connected herself in the New Desert through trees. The Old Ems had not had much previous experience with trees, and Sister Faye Mermaid was impressed that Sister Sheila Na Giggles Mermaid figured out the best thing to do for her was to be in this place: be here now.

Sister Faye Mermaid watched as Sister DeeDee Lightful Mermaid struggled at first. She was so accustomed to the milky watery depths. What was she going to do with all the light in the desert? Until she wandered the desert, listened to Coyote Woman, and later found her own light again. She became completely full of herself.

Sister Bea Wilder Mermaid had no idea what to do with herself in the New Desert, but she went out and learned the rhythms of the desert. She completely embraced the wild. Sister Lyra Musica Mermaid conquered her own fears and learned to live her siren song. Although Sister Laughs a Lot Mermaid lost her giggles for a time, she soon began belly laughing as she cultivated joy in the New Desert. And Sister Ursula Divine Mermaid came off the Mountains with a new name—and the ability to be at home in the world.

Sister Bridget Mermaid continued to encourage her own creative process, and Sister Faye Mermaid followed her example as they created songs and enchantments together—even though Sister Faye Mermaid did not feel the magic for a long while.

Sister Ruby Rosarita Mermaid was perhaps the most inspirational of all—even though Sister Faye Mermaid would certainly not rank them! Sister Ruby Rosarita Mermaid learned a new magic: She learned to cook. She transformed ingredients by cutting them up, heating them, cooling them, and/or whispering sweet some-things to them.

Sister Sophia Mermaid never stopped being wise, and she became even wiser, to Sister Faye Mermaid's way of thinking, because she came to understand the New Desert. Likewise, Sister Magdelene Mermaid was always full of love. That never changed.

Grand Mother Yemaya Mermaid was out to sea for a bit when they first arrived in the sandy realms. She soon learned to find her flow in the new world. And Mother Star Stupendous Mermaid continued to stare at the stars, honoring all that had come before them in every step she took.

Sister Faye Mermaid was impressed with her sister Old Mermaids. They had been tossed aside, as it were, tossed ashore in a new world, one they never asked for, one they never longed for, and yet they had all done their best. They had each risen to the occasion, more full of themselves, more knowledgeable, more capable than they had ever been.

As Sister Faye Mermaid walked the desert and contemplated all of this, she realized what was troubling her was that she did not understand what had happened. How had they landed here? Why? She listened to the coyotes and mockingbirds as she wandered. Listened to the whoosh, whoosh, whoosh as a crow flew overhead in the dry air. She stood in the wash where water sometimes ran, the Sometimes River, and she suddenly realized the reason they had landed here no longer mattered. They were here. They could not go back. She accepted the mystery of it all.

With this realization, her feet settled more deeply into the sand. She felt a breeze tickle the top of her head. And words began to fall from the blue sky, from cacti arms, from the beaks of passing birds. Sister Faye Mermaid felt enchantment all around her in the deep pulsing silence.

Sister Lyra Musica Mermaid and Magic Mateo

One day a man wandered into the Old Mermaids' Sanctuary with a huge bag flung over his shoulder. He was tall, dark, and gorgeous. At least, that's how Sissy Maggie described him when she came running into the house.

"And it looks like he's carrying someone in a bag!" Sissy Maggie said. "Could someone that pretty be carrying a dead body?"

"What?" Grand Mother Yemaya Mermaid said. "Where did you get such an idea?"

"The Pepperman and Pepperwoman told me bizarre things are happening beyond the Sanctuary and beyond the beyond," Sissy Maggie said.

Sister Sophia Mermaid rolled her eyes. "Sometimes the Old Neighbors are more full of stories than anything else."

The Old Mermaids all went outside to meet the visitor. Sister Lyra Musica Mermaid hung back a bit. If he had a body in his bag, she was not particularly eager to see it. She walked slowly as the other Old Ems surrounded the stranger. He set his pack on the table outside and quickly opened it. Some kind of yellow things fell out of it. The man smiled. The smile lit up his eyes. He glanced at Sister Lyra Musica Mermaid. She sucked her breath in slightly. He was good-looking.

"I am Mateo Brown," he said, gazing at Sister Lyra Musica Mermaid for a moment before turning his attention to the other Old Mermaids. "I've brought bananas!"

Bananas? Sister Lyra Musica Mermaid had heard of them. Some kind of sweet fruit.

"Magic Mateo," Sissy Maggie said. "I have heard of you. You bring sweetness wherever you go."

Magic Mateo smiled slightly. "I think it is the bananas that bring the sweetness. I am just their bagman."

The Old Mermaids all laughed. (They did not know what a bagman was; probably Magic Mateo didn't know either.)

"Splendid," Sister Ruby Rosarita Mermaid said. "I will make a chocolate sauce to go with them. And a feast to go with that."

"Come," Mother Star Stupendous Mermaid said. "Meet us all and join us. You are welcome. We will invite the neighbors so you can sell your bananas." Mother Star put her hand on Mateo's arm as they moved as a group toward the house. They were like butterflies around a flower. Or dragonflies around a small pretty pond. Sister Lyra Musica Mermaid stayed still. She did not know why. She could hear her heart in her chest. She wanted to see Mateo again, but looked away just as he glanced at her.

"I will go tell the neighbors," Sister Lyra Musica Mermaid said. She wasn't certain anyone heard her. She just wanted to get away. She wanted to stay, too, but she didn't understand why she was holding back. Why did she feel critical of her sister mermaids welcoming the new stranger?

Sister Lyra Musica Mermaid invited the Old Neighbors and invited them to invite anyone else. Then she ran home to find all the Old Mermaids involved in creating the feast. She glanced around but did not see Magic Mateo. Then suddenly someone tapped her shoulder. She turned around.

Mateo stood behind her. He really wasn't that tall. He smiled and put his index finger to his lips. Then he whispered, "Can you get me a bowl?"

Sister Lyra Musica Mermaid frowned. Then she said, "I can."

"And a fork."

Sister Lyra Musica Mermaid went into the kitchen, got a bowl from the cupboard and a fork from the drawer. Then she hurried back into what they called the gathering room. Mateo was still there. She handed him the bowl.

"Come with me," he said, "and I'll show you magic."

Sister Lyra Musica Mermaid glanced back toward the kitchen where her sisters were chatting and cooking. And then she followed Mateo outside. He set the bowl on the table next to the bananas. She stood across the table from him. He handed one banana to Sister Lyra Musica Mermaid and took one for himself.

"Please peel it and put it in the bowl," he said.

Sister Lyra Musica Mermaid watched him pull at the bottom of the fruit and pull away the peel. She imitated him and then they both dropped the bananas into the bowl.

"Now mash them down with the fork until you don't even recognize what they were," he said. "All the while think of healing nourishing delicious food."

Sister Lyra Musica Mermaid did what Mateo asked. He came around the table and stood next to her, watching as she pressed the fork into the flesh of the banana. Soon enough it was all gooey.

"Perfect." He reached into the bottom of the bag and pulled out two smaller bags. He opened one and poured flat oats over the bananas—about the same amount of oats as there were mashed bananas. He handed the other bag to her. "Add about half as much as the oats."

Sister Lyra Musica Mermaid opened the bag. Raisins! She poured some into the bowl. Mateo gently took the fork from her. "Now stir." He stirred a bit and then passed the fork back to Sister Lyra Musica Mermaid. She did the same.

"Now put about a tablespoon each on a baking tray in the oven for about 15-20 minutes and you will have the tastiest quickest cookies on the planet. This recipe is for exactly 13 cookies. One for each of the Old Mermaids."

"We need to make it 14 so you can have one," Sister Lyra Musica Mermaid said.

Mateo smiled. "Maybe you will give me half of yours?"

"Who says I'll share?" she asked.

They smiled at each other. Sister Lyra Musica Mermaid sighed. She felt herself relaxing for the first time in a long while.

"I feel like we met before," Mateo said. "Have we?"

"I-I don't know," she said. "I have forgotten so much since we left the Old Sea. Where are you from?"

He tilted his head to the east. "Over there."

She nodded. "And you take bananas and sell them to places like this?"

"Yes. And no. I do many things. I had a dream about

this place, and I had to come. I'm not sure why." He stared at her. He had dark brown eyes. "Maybe it was to make cookies with you."

She smiled. "We better get these into the oven before there's no room," she said.

They returned to the house together. She found a tray, and Mateo melded in with the Old Mermaids, talking easily to all of them. His conversation with her had been nothing special. Nor should it have been. Well, maybe it was special, but so were his other conversations with the other Old Mermaids. Sister Lyra Musica Mermaid dropped 13 potential cookies on the tray and then slipped it in the oven. When it was time, she took them out. The cookies had baked up nicely. They smelled vaguely of baked raisins. She put them on a plate and set them aside for later.

The Old Neighbors came from all around. They brought food and music. Everyone ate and danced. Magic Mateo told stories about traveling with a circus for awhile, living with a monk, and training horses for a rancher down south. He was quite the raconteur. Every time Sister Lyra Musica Mermaid saw Mateo, her heart seemed to beat a little faster, and she felt butterflies in her stomach. At least that was what the Witch told her it was called when she described it. The music was loud so they stepped a bit away from the dancers.

"I feel sort of scared and excited."

                                              Kim Antieau

"You've got butterflies," the Witch said. "It probably means you're in love."

"What does being in love mean?"

The Witch stared at her.

"I mean, I know what it is like to love. I love my sister mermaids. I love the Old Neighbors. I love the plants and animals. But what is being in love?"

"Hmmm. I'm not sure I can explain it. You want to be with someone all the time. You like to be touched by them. Usually it means you trust them—although sometimes that trust is betrayed. You want to have sex with them."

Sister Lyra Musica Mermaid frowned. "Have you been in love before?"

"Half a dozen times," she said. "If you're lucky, it's like a cold and goes away after a time, and you forget you ever caught it."

"I don't think that's it at all," Sister Lyra Musica Mermaid said.

The Witch shrugged. "Maybe you just ate something wrong."

Magic Mateo danced with everyone. Sister Lyra Musica Mermaid danced with everyone, too, except Mateo. She tried not to see him again. She didn't like the feeling in her stomach. But he was everywhere, it seemed, trying to catch her eye.

And then the night was over. As the Old Mermaids

cleaned up, Sister Lyra Musica Mermaid took the plate of cookies around. Each Old Em took one cookie until only one remained. She couldn't avoid Mateo any longer. After all, they were his cookies. She walked around the house and then went outside to find him sitting by the pool. She sat next to him. She held out the plate to him. He took the cookie. She set down the plate. He broke the cookie in half and gave her one half. Their hands touched briefly, and she felt a kind of electricity go down her arm. They looked at each other and then away again. They ate the cookie in silence.

"It's so good," Sister Lyra Musica Mermaid finally said. "How can three ordinary ingredients be so special?"

"The taste depends on the person mashing the bananas," he said.

She laughed. "Very funny."

"Every time you make them, I hope you'll think of me," he said. "In fact, just eat half. Leave the other half for me and I'll get the magic wherever I am."

"I feel strange around you. They call you Magic Mateo. Did you put a spell on me?"

"I feel strange around you, too," he said. "A good strange. Did you put a spell on me?"

"I wouldn't know how," Sister Lyra Musica Mermaid said.

"You are an Old Mermaid," he said. "Aren't you all

                                    Kim Antieau

magic? I can't stay long. I'm looking for something in particular."

"What is it?" she asked.

"I can't say," he said. "When I return, I hope I can tell you."

"When you return? You are coming back?"

"I hadn't intended to," he said. "But you and I just ate the same Thrice Magic Cookie. Technically we're married. Or at least we're bound to each other for life. I have to come back."

Sister Lyra Musica Mermaid laughed and leaned into Mateo. He leaned back.

"As long as there is a good reason," she said.

Magic Mateo stayed for three days and nights. Sister Lyra Musica Mermaid was with him most of the time. Although at night, he wandered away. He told her he turned into a pumpkin at night and didn't want any witnesses. She just laughed and watched him leave. She never noticed him looking for anything as she took him around the Sanctuary and beyond.

Then in the morning after the third night, the Old Mermaids said goodbye to their visitor. He had sold all of his bananas, yet his pack was full again of bananas.

"What magic is this?" Sister Faye Mermaid said under her breath.

Sister Lyra Musica Mermaid was the last to say goodbye. She held out her hand to him. He took her hand and kissed the top of it. Her stomach lurched. She moved closer to him, and they hugged.

"I wasn't joking when I said we are bound together," he said.

"Then don't go," Sister Lyra Musica Mermaid said. She suddenly felt again like she had when she lost the Old Sea. "Don't go." She wanted him to ask her to come with him. She couldn't go. Wouldn't go. Would she?

"I have to go," he said. He pulled away. His eyes were filled with tears. "One day I hope you'll understand."

And then he turned and walked away, dropping into the wash so she couldn't see him soon enough.

"So he was your butterflies," the Witch said, coming up next to Sister Lyra Musica Mermaid. "I hope you forget him soon. That is my wish for you."

"Never," Sister Lyra Musica Mermaid said.

Sister Lyra Musica Mermaid cried for days. She didn't understand how she felt. She couldn't eat. She ached to see Mateo again, just one more time, please, she begged the Cosmos. The Old Mermaids sang to her. Sisters Faye and Bridget Mermaid insisted this was some kind of magic or faery spell. Sisters Laughs a Lot Mermaid and Bea Wilder Mermaid said, "It's love. Leave her be."

Time went on, and Sister Lyra Musica Mermaid became herself again. She stopped watching for Mateo's return, and no one mentioned him around her. She did

                                        Kim Antieau

make the Thrice Magic Cookies every now again. 13 of them. She only ate half of hers. The other half she always left on the table in front of the house, where she and Mateo had made the first cookie batter. It was always gone in the morning. She knew some desert creature had made a meal of it. Still, she liked to imagine that somewhere Mateo got her magic some way or another and knew she was thinking of him.

The Cailleach

"The Cailleach made that mountain over there," the Witch of Coyote Hill said, pointing.

It was pitch black night. None of the Old Mermaids could see a thing except the stars above.

"She had a boulder all wrapped up in her apron to take home and decorate her yard," the Witch said. "So I heard. Then someone said something she didn't like, and she just dropped that boulder where it was. Not sure how many villages she wiped out. Maybe some. Maybe none."

"Oh my," Sissy Maggie said. "That doesn't sound good."

"Good or bad," the Witch said, "you gotta be careful talking about her or telling stories about her. I mean, what if I got a detail wrong? She might be striding over us right this second with a boulder about to drop from her apron."

"What does she look like?" Sister DeeDee Lightful Mermaid asked. "Would we know her if we saw her?"

"Of course," the Witch said. "I heard she has one eye, white hair, and blue skin. Blue like the coldest night blue."

"I bet she looks like the mountain," Sister Ursula Divine Mermaid said.

"Or the night sky," Mother Star Stupendous Mermaid suggested.

"I imagine she knows everything," Sister Sheila Na Giggles Mermaid said.

"Shhh," the Witch said. "I think I hear her outside."

"I don't hear anything," Sister Sheila Na Giggles Mermaid whispered. "Except the blinking of one eye."

Sister Lyra Musica Mermaid and the Cactus Wren

Sister Lyra Musica Mermaid was walking the wash and feeling as though she were filled up with anxiety and nothing else when she heard: "Hey, quit interrupting my song."

Sister Lyra Musica Mermaid looked around. She didn't see anyone who would understand her language. A cactus wren on top of a short saguaro was watching her.

"Yes, you," Cactus Wren said.

"I'm sorry," Sister Lyra Musica Mermaid said, "but I wasn't saying anything. How could I be interrupting your song?"

"Your thoughts, baby," Cactus Wren said. "Your entire vibe. Why are you so afraid? Look at me: I am literally standing on pins."

"You are literally standing on cactus needles."

"Pins, needles, what's the difference? You don't see me whining about it. Or being afraid of it. And see that hawk circling up there? It wants to end me dead, but I am gonna sing my song if it kills me."

Sister Lyra Musica Mermaid looked up. "And it might kill you. Why don't you hide until it's gone?"

"I might do that," Cactus Wren said. "And some days I do that. But today the sky is blue, these needles are sharp, and I want to sing my song."

"The hawk is gone," Sister Lyra Musica Mermaid said.

"There's always something else who wants to eat us," it said.

"How do you stand on those needles?"

"Very carefully," Cactus Wren said. "How do you walk on those legs?"

"Very carefully," Sister Lyra Musica Mermaid said. "So you know who we are. And who we were."

"Of course," Cactus Wren said. "Everyone knows. And, baby, we were all something else at one time."

Sister Lyra Musica Mermaid nodded. "That doesn't help me not be afraid."

Cactus Wren nodded. "Sometimes I am so afraid I shake in my boots."

Sister Lyra Musica Mermaid cocked her head, trying to imagine the cactus wren in boots.

"Metaphorically speaking," Cactus Wren said.

"What do you do when you are afraid?" Sister Lyra Musica Mermaid asked.

"I think of fear and anxiety as background noise," Cactus Wren said. "A kind of white noise that sometimes fills the Universe." The bird shrugged. "And then I sing. I mean, what else?"

"What else, indeed."

Cactus Wren opened its beak wide and said, "Top of the world, Ma!"

"Bottom of the world, Ma!" Sister Lyra Musica Mermaid said from her place in the wash.

"OK, OK, leave the singing to the professionals," Cactus Wren said.

"Really?"

"No, sing away. But sing away from here. I'm trying to find love. Nothing personal, but you're not my type."

Sister Lyra Musica Mermaid laughed. "I love you anyway. And I'm going to sing about it all day. Away, far away from here."

Finding Treasure

I got up and went to the tool box to get a nail. I leaned over and opened the red lid. It wasn't the toolbox. It was Grandpa Warren's fishing tackle box. I had gotten the wrong box. Another stupid move by me. I kicked the box. I kicked it harder than I intended and it flew across the room and slammed into the wall, scattering the contents of the top tray every which way across the attic floor.

Something fell out of the bottom of the box. Something sparkling, luminescent, something like a blue wave made of cloth. As the blue wave spilled onto the floor, a hush washed through the room—a hush filled with the songs of the stars, the whales, the sea. I felt time flutter.

I walked slowly over to the blue and sat on the floor next to it. The room whispered, Ahhhhhhh. It was a blue like blue I had never seen. It was a cloth like cloth I had never seen. It was as my grandmother had described it: It was the blue of a Santa Fe sky, the blue of the Earth from space, the blue of the most vibrant blue you'd ever seen. It was a blue that changed as I looked at it, as though the color itself was alive.

I knew exactly what it was.

I picked the blue up, cradled it in my arms, and carried it down the stairs.

I walked into the kitchen and held the blue cloth out to my grandmother.

"Here it is, Grandma," I said, "just like you said. I found where Grandpa hid it."

Everything in the world changed as soon as Grandma saw what was in my arms. She softened and strengthened all at the same time. She took it from me. She held part of it and let the rest fall away from her to the floor.

Mom gasped.

Grandma Merry wrapped the cloth around her, slowly, deliberately. It was as though I were watching a dream. And in this dream, my grandmother became herself again.

She held her arms out to us. Mom and I went to her and the three of us embraced.

I was like being hugged by a sea goddess.

Or an otter.

A bear.

A deer.

Snake.

Mountain.

River.

Grandma Merry looked at my mother. She put her hands on either side of my mom's face.

"Oh my darling Cara," she said. "You have grown into such a beautiful person. Look what you've done with your life. Those paintings of yours are exquisite. I really should have let you paint my portrait."

"I've always wanted to," Cara said. "There's still time. Two tails or one?"

Grandma Merry laughed. Oh what a laugh!

It was as if the real Merry had stepped into my grandmother's body after a long absence.

"I've always admired you, Cara," Grandmother Merry said. "You've lived your own life. You never let anyone take anything from you—except me. I'm sorry you never felt like you had a real mother. Probably because you didn't."

"You're real, Mom," she said.

Grandma Merry laughed again. "I am now."

She smoothed her hand down the blue. The color seemed to fill the room. Not like a sad blue, more like a sky blue, as if we were now a part of the sky.

"And you, my granddaughter," Grandma Merry said. She looked right into my eyes. "You are a wonderful person. We must help you to stop worrying so much about what other people think. Take off all the things other people try to put on you, take off all the things society tries to put on you, and just wear yourself. That's it. Wear your own skin, darlin'. We used to say, go with the flow, sister, and watch out for the waterfalls." Grandma Merry smiled at us. "I am so happy. Come, tell me all about your lives."

Sister Bridget Heals the World

One day, Sister Bridget Mermaid came upon a sparrow in the wash. It didn't fly away as she neared. In fact, it didn't move except for tilting its head now and again and looking stunned, the way a bird looks when it doesn't fly away. Sister Bridget Mermaid crouched in the sand near it. If it didn't fly away soon, some other creature was going to come by and eat it. If Sister Bridget Mermaid picked it up, she could harm it even more.

She began to softly sing. It was a lovely wordless song. She went through the vowels twice, and the bird cocked its head every time she sang, "Eh," so she sang it again and then again, playing with it, sometimes louder, sometimes softer. Until the bird seemed to yawn. Then it shivered, flapped its wings, and flew away.

Sister Bridget Mermaid smiled, stood, and then continued on her walk. When she told the story to the Old Mermaids later, Grand Mother Yemaya Mermaid said, "Sometimes it takes so much to heal the world, and sometimes it takes so little."

The Thirteen Suggestions

Get the starfish outta your eyes, sister.
Sister Sheila Na Giggles Mermaid

Step lightly. Dance hard. Eat your vegetables.
Sister DeeDee Lightful Mermaid

Things change. Get over it.
Sister Bea Wilder Mermaid

Fear has no sisters, but I have many.
Sister Lyra Musica Mermaid

She who laughs a lot laughs a lot.
Sister Laughs A Lot Mermaid

I am most at home where the wild things are.
Sister Ursula Divine Mermaid

Sing, dance, create. If you have to choose one, do all
three at once.
Sister Bridget Mermaid

A good bean is hard to find. Everything else is easy.
Sister Ruby Rosarita Mermaid

Go with the flow—and watch out for waterfalls.
Sister Sophia Mermaid

You ask me to tell you about love? Showing is so much
better.
Sister Magdelene Mermaid

Laugh or weep. We swim in your tears.
Grand Mother Yemaya Mermaid

All the wisdom of the ages can be distilled into one
suggestion: Be.
Mother Star Stupendous Mermaid

The rest is . . . mystery.
Sister Faye Mermaid

About the Author

Kim Antieau's novels include *Church of the Old Mermaids, Whackadoodle Times, The Fish Wife, The Jigsaw Woman, Coyote Cowgirl,* and many others. She lives in the Desert Southwest with the javelinas, lizards, roadrunners, coyotes, saguaros, bobcats, cactus wrens, and her husband, writer Mario Milosevic. www.kimantieau.com

The Old Ems are too marvelous for just one volume. In the following pages, Green Snake Publishing is proud to feature all of Kim's books in which the Old Mermaids bring their wisdom, charm, and sea smarts.

Every Old Mermaids book is available from your favorite independent bookstore and from online and ebook stores.

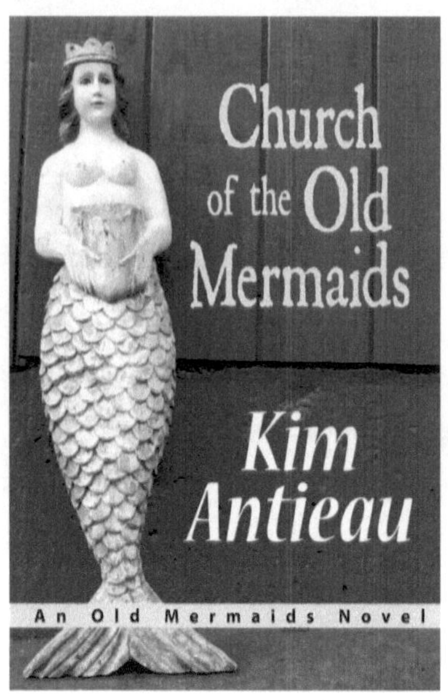

Myla Alvarez, novice, walks into the Sonoran desert near Tucson, Arizona, and begins telling stories about the Old Mermaids who were washed ashore onto the New Desert when the Old Sea dried up. In this mystical new world, they lived, created, and walked in beauty. Myla finds sustenance and meaning in their lives and stories. But she worries that Homeland Security may discover the undocumented migrants she harbors at the Old Mermaids Sanctuary. When an old friend reenters her life, Myla begins to doubt herself and the wisdom of preserving the Old Mermaids Sanctuary. Will the Old Mermaids come to her aid? *Church of the Old Mermaids* is a tale of redemption, love, compassion, and mystery.

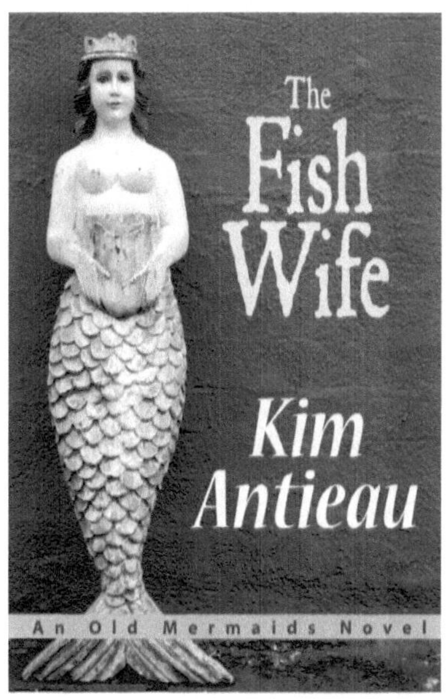

Sara O'Broin loves life in her Irish village. But when an ancient curse decrees she must be a fish wife to a man she does not love, she risks everything—including her own life—on a perilous ocean journey to the New World. Seeking to break the curse and live life on her own terms, she finds the world outside her village holds danger and wonder. With the Old Mermaids by her side, her epic quest for freedom takes her to a land and community full of mystery, magic, and a life she never expected.

Serena Blue lives for one thing: to spend time with her boyfriend. She can't stand the stories of the Old Mermaids her mother constantly tells, and she suspects her own family's sanity when she learns her grandmother believes she once lived as a mermaid. Lost and unsure of where her life will lead, Serena casts about for something to believe in. When the truth of her grandmother's past surfaces, Serena must struggle for her own survival and uncover the difference between reality and delusion.

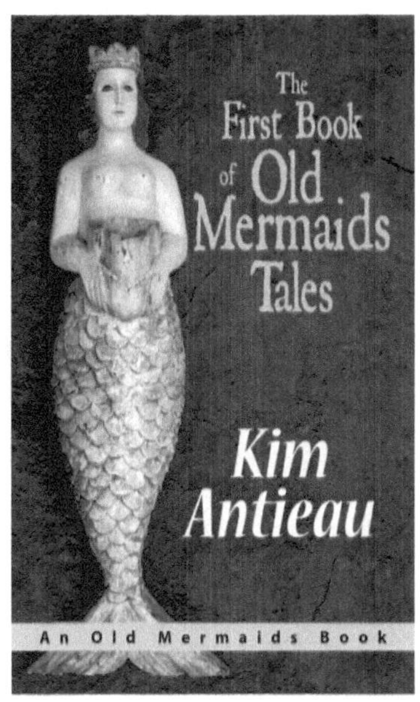

When the Old Sea dries up, the Old Mermaids find themselves washed up on the New Desert. These tales of the Old Mermaids remind us of the beauty all around us, even on those days when we wonder how we'll survive, let alone thrive. Sister Ruby Rosarita Mermaid brews a magical story-telling soup to bring peace. A mysterious stranger brings the Old Mermaids an elixir to heal all. And then there's the Tea Shell, where the Old Mermaids serve the most marvelous teas. The Old Mermaids support one another, love their new world, and build community with all their human and nonhuman neighbors. You can be assured when you stop by the Tea Shell for a cup of Essence of Coyote Laughter Tea that no coyotes were harmed in the making of your brew.

Are you feeling overloaded? Surrounded by chaos? Or maybe you're no longer sure what your purpose is. Perhaps you've never known. In a world of noise and chaos, *The Old Mermaids Mystery School* offers simple steps to connect with Nature, our true selves, and each other. Each Mystery in *The Old Mermaids Mystery School* features the wisdom of one of the Old Mermaids. You won't find any dogma, religion, or exams here. Instead, revel in each of the 13 Mysteries, revealed to you over time, taking you from Sister Sheila Na Giggles Mermaid's practical steps on being in the here and now to Sister Faye Mermaid's "The rest is mystery."

The Old Mermaids bring their wisdom to you in *The Old Mermaids Oracle*, a practical tool for navigating life's ever-changing circumstances.

This book was originally only available to novices of The Old Mermaids Mystery School. It is now available to all. This small guidebook is for your use once you make your own set of oracles. Or you can use the book itself as the oracle by asking a question and flipping the pages until you stop on an Old Mermaid entry.

In the guidebook to *The Old Mermaids Wisdom Cards*, the Old Ems reveal the secrets of living life to the fullest in 65 lush cards featuring Kim Antieau's stunning photographs. The Wisdom Cards do not predict the future or tell you the ultimate fate of your soul. Instead, use the cards to find your true self right now, your true purpose in the here and now, and how to live with a wild and generous heart for the benefit of you and your community.

The guidebook is available wherever books and ebooks are sold. You can buy the Old Mermaids Wisdom Card decks here: https://tinyurl.com/4cnd2wzr

This journal may or may not be based on the original journal of one or more of the Old Mermaids living in the Old Mermaids Sanctuary. The legend goes that whatever anyone draws or writes on these pages brings healing, joy, and magic into the world and into the life of the person who owns the journal. This journal alternates blank and lined pages and has quotes from *Church of the Old Mermaids* on every page.

MAGIC, MYTH, AND MERRYMAKING

13 Days of Yuletide the Old Mermaids Way

Kim Antieau

Join the Old Mermaids for their annual celebration of all things wild and marvelous with 13 days of beauty, meditations, recipes, creative prompts, myths, magic, and Old Mermaid tales. All designed to usher in the New Year with joy, creativity, and love.

Magic, Myth, and Merrymaking comes in three versions: a gorgeous full color edition (perfect for gift giving) a handsome black and white edition, and an ebook edition. You can access all three on the Amazon page by clicking on the "see all formats and editions" link.

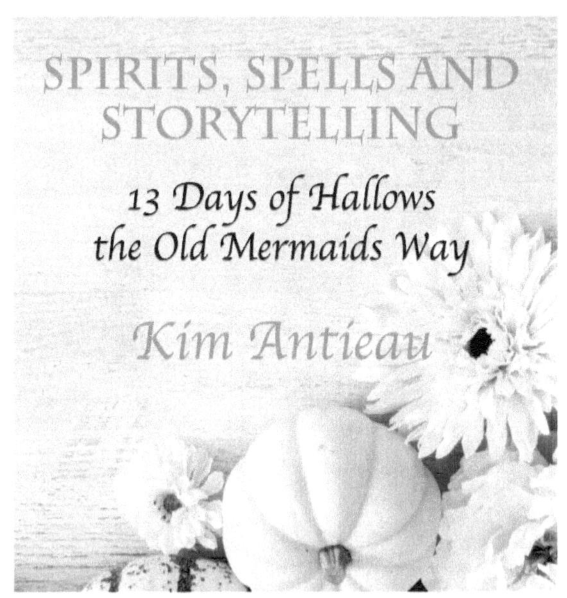

Join the Old Mermaids for their annual celebration of all things wild and marvelous with 13 days of beauty, meditations, food, creative prompts, myths, magic, and Old Mermaid tales. All designed to celebrate Hallows/Samhain the Old Mermaids way.

Spirits, Spells, and Storytelling comes in three versions: a gorgeous full color edition (perfect for gift-giving) a handsome black and white edition, and an ebook edition. You can access all three on the Amazon page by clicking on the "see all formats and editions" link.

Kim Antieau guides you through a year of wisdom, humor, beauty, inspiration, and love in these daily quotes from her own writings featuring the Old Mermaids and some of the other wise and mystical characters from her books and stories. See what gifts Grand Mother Yemaya Mermaid, Sister Laughs A Lot Mermaid, Mother Star Stupendous Mermaid, Sister Sheila Na Giggle Mermaid, and others have to share with you all year long.

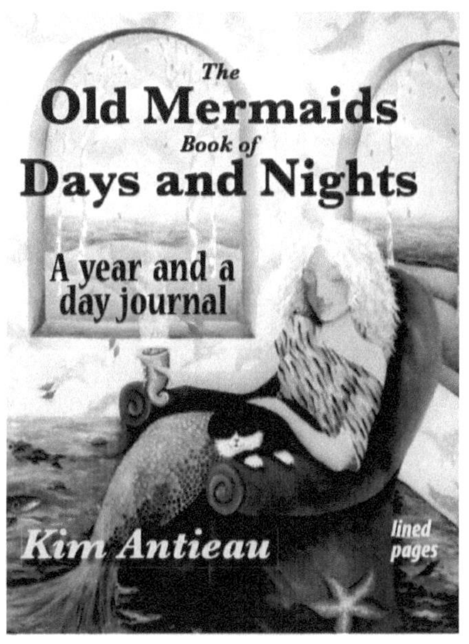

We love *The Old Mermaids Book of Days and Nights*—filled with quotes, one for every day of the year—so much that we decided to make a companion for it: a BIG sumptuous luxurious "a year and a day" journal. This 8.5 x 11 book has the same cover as *The Old Mermaids Book of Days and Nights*, but we've removed the dates so you can put in your own and we've made one journal lined and one unlined; you can use both for journals or use one for a journal and one for sketching or mix and match. A Year and A Day is a traditional period of time set aside for study or initiation, and you can begin any time. We hope you will find these journals inspiring and beautiful. This is a perfect place to tell your own story and find your siren song.

Church of the Old Mermaids celebrates its fifteenth birthday with a brand new edition of this beloved novel. A glorious celebration of life, love, friendship, and the power to change, *Church of the Old Mermaids* challenges us to find the good in others and ourselves. This edition is fully annotated by Kim Antieau and Mario Milosevic, illuminating the sources of the Old Mermaids and bringing new understanding and depth to this classic novel of souls adrift seeking a secure shore in a world of peril and uncertainty.

Myla Alvarez, novice, walks into the Sonoran Desert and begins telling stories about the Old Mermaids who washed ashore onto the New Desert when the Old Sea dried up. In this mystical new world, they lived, created, and walked in beauty. Myla finds sustenance and meaning in their lives and stories. But she worries that Homeland Security may discover the undocumented migrants she harbors at the Old Mermaids Sanctuary. When an old friend reenters her life, Myla begins to doubt herself and the wisdom of preserving the Old Mermaids Sanctuary. Will the Old Mermaids come to her aid?

Full of magic yet rooted in the cruel and beautiful realities of the border and those who live near it, this new presentation of *Church of the Old Mermaids* is sure to please both new and old readers of this unique and still timely novel.

This new edition also contains an introduction by Mario Milosevic and three essays on mermaids and storytelling by Kim.

A special book deserves a special cover, and we are fortunate to have an exclusive and stunning image by the extraordinary artist Charles Vess for this edition of *Church of the Old Mermaids.*

The Annotated Church of the Old Mermaids is available in hardcover, paperback, and as an ebook.